Ge
over t
Pengu
Past
show.

He
Ross,
Ian H
famo
spotte
them

He
bands
them'
Roya
Olym

Mo
'Cat
exasp
world

Geo
succe
Geoff
the fi
prone

In order to mak   otal
of eight novels fo   r as
he grows up an   nily
wonders if he wil

A Nasty Bump on the Head
Geoff Tristram

A Comedy of Errors

DRAWING
ROOM

First published in 2005 by the Drawing Room Press

(A part of Geoff Tristram Limited)

Second Printing 2007

Revised Third Printing 2008

Fifth Anniversary Edition 2010

Printed and bound in Great Britain by
CPI Antony Rowe, Chippenham and Eastbourne

Contact the author on gt@geofftristram.co.uk

ISBN 978-0-9551428-0-2

Cover illustration, 'David and Miss Kettle' by Geoff Tristram.

I wrote this story five years ago, and it was my first ever attempt at comedy writing, so I had a lot to learn. For instance, the initial draft saw David leaving for school on a Monday morning, but returning home on a Friday evening. There were typographical and punctuation errors everywhere too. I painstakingly corrected them all, only to discover that loads of new ones had sneaked into the book that same evening, as I slept. However, over the last five years, I have learnt quickly, and now I am easily as good as, say, William Shakespeare or P.G. Wodehouse, as you will notice when you read my newer stuff.

Strangely, in spite of this, people seem to genuinely love this first book, and it still sells really well, even now. I love it too, and that's why I've decided to get it a present for its birthday. I've been through it again with a fine-toothed comb, weeding out the mistakes that had leapt back into it while I wasn't looking, and tidying up the odd awkward sentence (I didn't go too mad or there'd have been nothing left). I also painted a new cover for it, because the old one didn't match the house style I'd created with my second attempt, Monet Trouble, which always features David himself, either in a state of deep distress or embarrassment. He only ever seems to have two facial expressions, which probably says a lot about my drawing skills too.

It's been a lot of effort, but it's the least I can do for an old and dear friend that got me started as a writer.

Now I need to recoup some money to pay for these changes, so would you mind forking out for this new edition please, even if you have the old version? I'd be ever so grateful!

Love, Geoff Tristram

"His purse is empty already;
all his golden words are spent."

Hamlet

That's used up another page.

CHAPTER 1

The Tempest

Brierley Bank, November 6th 1965

Eleven-year-old David Day was scraping the baked beans off his hamster when his mother called him in for breakfast.

Perhaps it's best to rewind just a little, to five minutes earlier. That opening sentence made him sound a little strange, which was a teeny bit unfair. He was, after all, just a normal little boy who seemed to find himself constantly embroiled in bizarre situations that were often not of his making. He appeared to have a knack of attracting them, like a human 'bizarre situations magnet', if indeed there is such a thing.

His dad had just gone into his garden shed, where he spent hours making things out of wood. This was his little bit of therapy after a hard day at the factory, where he spent hours making things out of metal. He had called his son to come in and take a look at something, and David could tell from his dad's tone that all was not well. The lad had been busy reducing his cycle-speedway bike to a mound of cogs, bearings, springs and chain links, blissfully untroubled by how they would eventually reassemble, when his dad's urgent voice cut through the crisp November air.

David wiped a filthy, oil-stained hand down the Fair Isle jumper which his loving mother had spent weeks knitting for him, and ran in the direction of the shed. His hamster, Jennings, the cause of his dad's concern, was as stiff as a board and showing no interest whatsoever in his lunch, which was unusual. Never one for *haute cuisine*, rich foods and fancy sauces, nevertheless Jennings was always at the table, knife and fork poised, eager to stuff his little face. Apart from this particular morning, that is. Having never experienced death first hand, David was shocked, to say the least. He vaguely realized that hamsters didn't reach three score and ten, but for five bob, he'd expected its company for a while longer. His dad carefully and respectfully removed him from his bed, (the hamster's bed, that is, not David's dad's bed) and they stood silently for a second or two. Coming from a council property, and not having money to burn, (David's dad, not the hamster) he quickly dismissed David's initial suggestion of a large state funeral or cremation, attended by all of the extended family, and opted for the galvanized metal bin in the back yard. He explained to David that it was what Jennings would have wanted. No fuss.

It's quite uncanny how 'what the deceased would have wanted' somehow always coincides exactly with what is convenient for the relatives. Strange, that.

Being a typical eleven-year-old boy, David's unbearable grief subsided at precisely the same time that the idea of a new, and hopefully more robust pet was suggested. He dried the tears and perused his 'Observer Book of Domestic Animals' for Mark Two, whom he'd already resolved to christen Darbishire. Meanwhile, his mother busied herself clearing away the breakfast things, scraping plates, washing up, and saying 'there there' to her gentle-natured offspring, whose freshly-shed tears had made the filthy oil stains on his face run, giving him the look of one of those pathetic little children who virtually lived up chimneys in Charles Dickens's books. He turned to the page on hamsters, and was contemplating the wisdom of spending hard-earned pocket-money on another of these fragile creatures, when he saw a paragraph that caught his eye. It stated:

'Sometimes, if the weather is cold, hamsters can go into hibernation. Their heart-rate slows down and the body stiffens. To the inexperienced owner, the animal can appear dead, but before presuming that this is the case, wrap the hamster in some bedding near (but not too near) to a fire in your house, and it may well wake up from its winter sleep.'

There was more, but there lay the nub. David was horrified. Imagine if he'd gone for the state funeral, or even worse, the cremation. He dashed outside and carefully removed the sorry creature from the bin. Jennings, trusty companion of six months, was covered in cold baked beans and bits of carrot scrapings - not a dignified end, even if it only cost five bob. A squeamish youngster at the best of times, David bit the bullet and began the vile task of cleaning up this potential mini-corpse.

It was at this juncture, one will recall, that his mother called him from inside the house to inform him that it was time to get off to school. David ran inside with his tomato-stained pet, stuffed him into a sock that he'd purloined from his mother's washing basket and lay him down gently by the gas fire. He had not yet eaten breakfast, and only having ten minutes to do so, he elected to give the baked beans a miss and instead opt for the toast and marmalade. He sat by the window and wolfed down his food, all the time keeping a weather-eye on the cadaver in the sock for signs of resuscitation.

It was then that a remarkable thing happened. All of a sudden, there was a mighty gushing sound, like a whirlwind. A pile of sand that his dad had been using to lay slabs in the garden simply disappeared without trace, whilst two single-car garages and a large potting shed took off into the air and sailed straight over the neighbour's houses, completely intact. The galvanized bin that so nearly became the final resting place for Jennings was now upended in the next door neighbour's fish pond, and the little creatures not killed instantly or traumatized by the impact were introduced to the gastronomic delights of cold baked beans and carrot scrapings, which probably made a nice change from gnats.

And then, silence.

An eerie, strange silence, eventually punctuated by puzzled cries of 'what on *earth* was that?' and 'did you see what I just saw?' from stunned neighbours outside. Inside, neither mom nor dad had seen or heard a thing, as they were preoccupied with the recent events at the foot of the gas fire.

Jennings, refreshed and now wide-awake, had legged it out of the sock, disappeared into the ventilation hole under the gas fire, and was steadfastly refusing to meet his public or sign autographs. Perhaps he had come to the conclusion - and who could blame him - that it would be better to offer his services to a family that refrained from making decisions best left to qualified vets, and wouldn't dispose of him or smear him in tomato sauce just because he fancied a bit of an extended lie in.

Life, which had previously been predictable and rather mundane, now had too many things going on at once. Given the 'look for Jennings' or 'find the garages' options, and being somewhat pushed for time, David chose the latter. He ran out onto the main road to see all three buildings, still intact, though decidedly shaky-looking, randomly arranged in the road and bewildering the traffic. The sand pile did not materialize, and is probably, for all we know, still circling the globe, like a lost soul.

Unable to fully enjoy the spectacle due to the urgency of school, David retired inside to put on his school shoes and tie, a routine that was always carried out as he sat in the comfy armchair in the corner of the back room - except on Fridays, which was washing day. On Fridays, the chair was temporarily removed to the front room and substituted for a large enamelled bath full of hot, soapy water, with which his mother did something mysterious, aided by two bleached sticks held together with a metal spring. They may have been called boiler sticks; they may not. These details were of no concern to the average eleven-year-old boy, who thought clothes were washed and ironed by pixies.

It was into this vat of extremely hot, soapy water that he now sat, rather heavily and in full school uniform, a shoe in each hand. Those who have dropped a four-ton boulder into a canal will know what the room looked like at that precise moment. David emitted a scalded wail, like a cat that had - for want of a better analogy - fallen heavily into an enamelled tub of hot water. His dad, who was slurping his final cup of tea prior to dashing off to his tool-making job, felt the full weight of the tidal wave. The gallon or so that hit David's mother in the small of her back as she carried a pile of washing over to the clotheshorse came as such a shock that she fell against the door and banged her head. The television, which didn't want to be left out of the action, chose this precise moment to add to the mayhem by

5

imploding in protest against being drenched, sending broken glass and thick blue smoke all over the room, and it was a miracle that no one was killed. It must be stressed yet again that the poor child was not personally responsible for *all* of the day's happenings, but his presence somehow served as a catalyst. That was the only way to explain it.

David was late for school that day, but rather than offer a detailed explanation, which he felt could potentially waste the remainder of the day, he took the detention and deduction of points for Yellow House like a man. Having completely missed assembly and English, he settled into the second lesson of the morning, which was Geography, thinking to himself that he'd had at least a year's worth of entertainment and it was still only ten-past ten. They say it comes in threes, and by fair reckoning he was all done and dusted. He wrote a quick list on the back of his Geography notebook.

David Day (Aged 11)

Exciting things that have happened today so far. Friday 6th November 1965.

1. Hamster Resurrection.
(Maybe, if we ever meet again, I should rename him Jesus.)

2. Tornado.

3. Flood.

Our topic in Geography today is Earthquakes.

CHAPTER 2

Day Dreaming

Mr Lewis, Geography teacher and Deputy Head, was a young athletic-looking Welshman, well liked by the pupils. He ran a tight ship and kept his little darlings in line with Cinderella, who resided in his bottom drawer. She was a tartan size-nine slipper that had long since retired from her job of keeping the teacher's right foot warm, and was nowadays kept busy dusting the backsides of wayward or unruly pupils. Shortly after the slipper had survived a recent kidnap attempt, Mr Lewis was prompted to remind the children that Cinderella's identical friend, Prince Charming, was waiting at home for *his* chance to see some action, and he, the teacher explained with a glint in his eye, was *far* more enthusiastic about his new role than Cinderella had ever been.

This not only seemed to stop the mini-crime wave dead in its tracks, but also taught the pupils an invaluable lesson in life; namely, 'better the devil you know'.

Mr Lewis wrote energetically on the blackboard, the chalk banging away like a Bonfire Night Jumping Jack, with fragments showering all over the floor beneath.

EARTHQUAKES.

He spun round to address the class, in his Richard Burton Welsh brogue.

"Quiet please. Now, before we get cracking, did anyone experience that strange whirlwind affair this morning? It blew my garden trellis up in the air and smashed it into a hundred pieces."

Ten or so eager hands bolted skywards, accompanied by a cacophony of "Sir, sir, me sir!"

He chose, rather unwisely it must be said, Craig Evans to chip in with his personal recollection of the freak wind.

"Sir, sir, my dad was walking down to the shed and it blew him off his feet and he landed on his arse, sir!"

"That's quite enough of that kind of language, Master Evans," insisted Mr Lewis, moving on swiftly. "David. You have your hand up. What happened to you then?"

"Sir, the wind made all of my dad's sand disappear, and it blew three garages over our house and into the main road sir!"

The classroom erupted with laughter.

"Steady on, young David," smiled his teacher. "It was hardly a full-blown hurricane, lad."

David flushed red, inwardly seething with resentment because no one had believed him.

"Right-o then!" continued Mr Lewis, sensing the boy's righteous indignation and not wishing to upset one of his favourite pupils. "Turn to page twenty-six in your geography textbooks. This morning's event leads us very nicely into our topic for the day. We've been examining the various natural phenomena that Mother Earth throws at us, such as clouds, rainbows, monsoons and so on. Young Master Day, being as you're already on your feet, you can do the first reading for us. From the top of the page. Nice big voice. Earthquakes, if you please!"

David was a good reader, and wasn't usually concerned in the least by public speaking, unlike poor Terry Deakin in the corner, who had a terrible speech impediment that mangled his 'R's and 'L's. He reluctantly put his righteous indignation to one side for five minutes, cleared his throat, opened his geography book to the right page and launched confidently into it.

"It is easy to be mizzled by earthquake statistics."

David looked puzzled. He could make nothing of this. He tried to clear his head and took another stab at it.

"It is easy to be mizzled…"

No. That word was a new one. It meant nothing to him.

Meanwhile, the steady trickle of superior laughter was becoming a serious burst pipe. Mr Lewis, usually the soul of discretion when it came to embarrassing his delicate young charges, ejected a strange pneumatic, snorting noise through his nose, and his face turned a very strange shade of Alizarin Crimson. This was how he expressed amusement. David, who obviously had a bright future ahead of him as The Human Chameleon, matched Mr Lewis's colour exactly within a second, presumably so that he could imitate his immediate surroundings and disappear.

"Okay, that's enough, you lot," shouted the teacher. "It's not so easy when you're up there, in front of the class. The word is *misled,* David. You've probably never seen it written down before. Sit down son, you've gone hot!"

9

As embarrassments went, it was fairly minor. It was far worse the week before, when Mr Lewis, not realizing that Deakin was quite so afflicted in the tonsil department, asked him to stand and read from his mathematics textbook the new word, COROLLARY.

The poor chap took a good long run at it, came out with 'Cowowwawee' and it took till playtime to slipper away all the stray giggles. At the tender age of eleven, embarrassment was a daily problem. It could take the form of a question to teacher, arm raised high and supported by the other arm, but accidentally pre-fixed with 'mom' instead of 'sir'. That could make even the hardest little tough-guy types wilt instantly with shame. Another good one was complete loss of bowel control, which could be, on occasion, spectacular. Until he had seen it with his own eyes, Mr Lewis could not believe what a small child could produce from such a tiny waste management system.

David Day was very easily embarrassed, and he had taken this latest slight on his otherwise excellent reading abilities very badly. In fact, once he had returned to his seat, dazed, he began to take very little part in the proceedings. His mind began to wander, and events around him were now no more than a blur. He was a notorious daydreamer at the best of times, but this cringeworthy public speaking attempt had sent him deeper into one of his trances. He began to ponder the fate of Jennings, and the likelihood of him being able to fend for himself in the wild - if the back of the gas fire could be described as the wild. He may well have been prepared, with cheek pouches stocked up and ready for his adventure. He may not. At a push, reasoned David, he could crane his neck round and perhaps lick a bit of the baked bean sauce off his back to keep him going. That was if he could stomach the stuff. David didn't care much for it, but then again, he'd never been stuck behind a gas fire, starving. Maybe he could even bring himself to eat beetroot under those conditions, and he *hated* beetroot.

His daydream began to change course, and now David became preoccupied with the rebuilding of his stricken cycle-speedway bike. Originally, he had been looking into the possibility of fixing a folded-up cigarette packet to his back wheel. This would catch the spokes as they rotated, giving a pleasingly realistic motorcycle-engine sound. All the kids on the estate were getting them, and he didn't want to be left out. This led to him noticing that his gear hub was filthy, which in turn prompted him to dismantle it, and from there things had got steadily worse. He was pondering how he could get all the ball bearings back inside the wheel, when, out of the fog he vaguely heard Mr Lewis talking about changing for P.E. Instantly snapping out of his reverie, David began pulling his school jumper over his head and undoing his tie, eager not to be the last one in the room to be ready, for a change. Brierley Bank Junior School often didn't bother to use their changing rooms, and pupils just took their clothes off in class, leaving a neat pile of clothing on their desks. At that age, there wasn't any awkwardness about undressing in mixed company. That came at the big school later, when girls began to grow breasts and boys developed embarrassing hairs. Life was hard for the girls that had developed early, and even more so for Simon Fisher. He'd had hairs *and* breasts for ages.

David removed his school shirt and vest, and unhooking his red and green snake belt, slipped down his short trousers to the ankles. He became aware of Mr Lewis's voice, very, very close to his right ear. It had a conspiratorial, hushed tone to it. David also thought he could detect a backing track of stifled snorts.

"David, what are you doing, son?"

"Getting changed for P.E., sir."

"And can I ask, why you are getting changed for P.E., and virtually stark naked, whilst the rest of the class continue with their arithmetic lesson?"

This unexpected new line of questioning had rather thrown him. He cautiously began to look around the room, and thirty fully-clothed arithmetic students sniggered back at him, hands clasped to their mouths. Some collapsed in helpless laughter. Others just stared in disbelief.

"Er, didn't you ask us to, erm …change for P.E., sir?" gulped the poor soul with tremulous voice, whilst simultaneously putting in a fast-track plea to the Almighty for a real-life earthquake to swallow him up.

"No David. I may have said at some point that P.E. was to follow after sums, that's all. Would you prefer to stay looking like a television wrestler, or shall I help you back on with your clothes?"

The deeply embarrassed young fellow began to get dressed again. His friend, Malcolm, (affectionately known as Mally Lobes) who sat next to him, gave him a friendly dig in the ribs and commented, in what was presumably meant to be a complimentary manner, "You're a flippin'NUTTER!"

David continued the lesson with his head so close to his exercise book that he couldn't focus. He could feel the tears welling up, which he occasionally dried with the cuff of his shirt when he thought no one was looking. All eye contact was avoided until the end of lesson bell sounded, and there was enough energy coming from his cheeks to heat a small Welsh village in February. With his vision still blurred, he quietly added a footnote to his list of the day's excitements.

No earthquake as yet. Pity.

The rest of the day passed mercifully without incident. He spent lunchtime with Malcolm over the banks beside the school, collecting spent skyrockets from the previous night's bonfire celebrations.

In the afternoon, as was his wont of a Friday, he worked on his plywood sheep in the woodwork room.

David was, by far, the most talented artist at his school, which probably explained his sensitive nature. In fact, so precocious were his talents that the Headmaster, Mr Perriman, had chosen him to create three sheep for use in the end of term Nativity play. This practical-minded head teacher realized that using real sheep would be problematic in numerous ways, and it occurred to him that a matching set, or flock, of hardy plywood sheep would be just the job. They would provide his three designated shepherds with a *raison d'etre*, and last for many years, thrilling adults and children alike, if stored correctly and regularly serviced. It would also keep one of his more scatterbrained boys quiet, and leave him only two hundred or so more to worry about.

David had been given the task nice and early - in September to be precise - and he was still happily jig-sawing his way halfway round sheep number one, with blades breaking at an average of one every three inches. As a trusted senior boy, he was left largely to his own devices, except when Miss Evans, the school secretary, popped in to see how many boxes of blades she would need to order for the following week. Occasionally, Mr Perriman himself would drop by, and remark to young David that he could have purchased a whole flock of the real things for less than these three had cost him, which made them very special sheep indeed. David thanked him profusely.

In response to Mr Perriman's query about the completion date, and his slight concern that The Nativity play was traditionally better suited to Christmas than the following July, the lad assured him that all three would be on time, as long as the blade supply held out.

Progress that particular afternoon was good, because David's dad had been trying to improve his son's jigsaw technique in the shed over the weekend, and the lesson had reaped dividends. At this rate of improvement, a blade would begin to last for half a sheep soon, and the school could use the funds saved to buy a badly needed new roof.

At twenty to four, David put his saw away, took off his apron and quickly returned to his classroom, just in time to join his colleagues in the mysterious and largely pointless ritual known as 'placing chairs on tables and standing silently till the bell goes.' Nor did that old and trusted brass retainer let them down. Cometh the hour, cometh the bell, bang on time, and total silence gave way to three hundred and fifty screaming banshees, desperate to let off steam.

David grabbed his satchel and pump bag, ran out of the school quadrangle and through the front entrance to the high street. Outside it was already almost dark, and the traditional post-bonfire night fog was descending over Brierley Bank. Children streamed off in all directions, back to the cosy glow of their little homes, their 'real flame effect' gas fires, Heinz Tomato Soup and Blue Peter. Tired factory workers in donkey jackets and West Bromwich Albion scarves chugged by on red double-decker buses, and the tiny, Victorian shop fronts were all lit up, their owners sipping tea and dealing with the last customers of the day. Brierley Bank at teatime was Under Milk Wood, a Lowry painting and a Charles Dickens novel, all rolled into one, as its good people returned to their loved ones after a hard day's work.

David wasn't going home that evening, however.

CHAPTER 3

The Fog

David had managed to remember that this was the night he had to go straight to Freddy Fielding's Barber Shop from school and onwards to his grandparents' house for tea afterwards. Often, he'd completely forget and arrive home, to be met with his long-suffering mother's usual greeting, "What on earth are we going to do with you?"

Tonight, his mother would have been proud of him. He'd even remembered what the few shillings in his left-hand trouser pocket were for. Remembering the barbers was one thing. Remembering not to spend the barber's fee on sweets at lunchtime was quite another. The money currently burning a large hole in his right-hand pocket, however, was for something altogether less prosaic than a haircut. This was the sum total of three weeks' accumulation of pocket money, with which he was intending to purchase a model aeroplane from Kettle's Toy and Joke Shop, in an effort to diminish the mental suffering caused by what he knew would be a severe and unflattering new hairstyle. The toy would also partly compensate for the anguish of having to deal with Miss Kettle herself.

David pulled up his collar to protect himself as best he could from the chilly, damp air and paused at the zebra crossing outside the school until Barbara, the roly-poly crossing lady, gave him and the other twenty or so children permission to cross.

Barbara was a kindly middle-aged woman, adored by all the children. She knew all of their names by heart, and probably where most of them lived. Weighing at least eighteen stone, but short in stature, she looked as if she had been poured into her crossing lady uniform, and someone had forgotten to say 'when!' Her arms, which were modelled on those of Mrs Mills, the television pianist, were thicker than a wrestler's thighs, and could only have got that way by their owner being force-fed every day since birth like a French goose, only with wheelbarrow-loads of bread pudding and chocolate éclairs instead of corn. A tailor's tape measure would have struggled to make ends meet around her upper arm, and any sudden movement from those gigantic structures could have caused a ripple effect in the under-hanging fatty areas which would have proved nigh-on impossible to bring under control; a potential tidal wave, or tsunami, of human blubber that could potentially gather momentum and become an unstoppable force. There must have been something in the water around the Black Country that helped form these huge-armed, pinafore-clad bruisers - there were more per square-mile than anywhere else in the country.

As David crossed, eyes glued to Barbara's heroic proportions, he indulged in his favourite fantasy; the one where he would produce, as if from nowhere, a meat cleaver and deliver a deft blow to her upper arm, completely and cleanly severing it to expose a prime cut of beef like the ones on display in the many high street butcher's shops.

There was no intended malice whatsoever in this. He was just a little boy blessed - or maybe cursed - with a *very* fertile and vivid imagination.

Once safely across the busy main road, David skipped up to the door of Freddie Fielding's Barber Shop. He paused nervously, as if about to be subjected to some awful ritual humiliation, which of course he was, and rehearsed his speech out aloud.

"Please Mr Fielding, Mom said, can you leave my sideburns on?" adding rather cryptically, "Please God, don't let him set fire to my head this time, Amen."

Taking a deep breath, he pushed the door. A bell clanged and he shuffled in, sheepishly taking a seat. Inside, six men and one forlorn boy were sat in a row, waiting for Freddie. Most of them had come straight from work, which almost certainly meant the local chain-making shops or metal-bashing factories. They chatted in broad Black Country accents, or browsed at their grubby pink Sports Argus newspapers. Most wore donkey jackets and flat caps, which were especially useful for disguise after one of Freddie's haircuts. The boy, whom David recognized as 'Gig Lamps' from across Woodland Avenue, (christened thus because of his overly-large spectacles) was engrossed in his Eagle comic. The front cover showed a particularly dramatic painting of the Mekon astride his personal flying saucer and, as ever, intent on doing Dan Dare a bit of no good.

Freddie Fielding was holding court. A dapper man of around sixty, dressed in a grey nylon overall with the top pocket displaying the tools of his trade, he fired brusque questions at his sitter.

"See the Albion on Saturday, John?"

"Ar! Rubbish, as usual wor they, Fred."

"Do you want Brylcreem?"

"Ar, Fred."

"And do you want to be singed?"

"Better had, Fred. Keep the cold out."

Men of few words, these chainmakers, but each word was bellowed seemingly not from the mouth, but from a hidden speaker somewhere near the chest. The deafening volume, which they had had to develop in order to be heard above the crashing and pounding hammers, was quite a shock in the church-like quiet of a barber's shop. Copious quantities of dirty hair hit the brown linoleum floor, as each client was dispatched. Freddie was of the old school. He knew but one style, and that was what you got. You could ask - nay beg - for a Tony Curtis, or, if you preferred, a Roger Moore, but what you ended up with was a Freddie Fielding - short back and sides.

He always began by applying some vigorous snipping to the top of the head, the tiny scissors working their magic at an alarming rate. Throughout this period, he would fire off staccato questions about the government, the Albion's latest performance and the cost of living. No matter what his sitter's name was, he was referred to as John. This sound piece of logic saved Freddie the embarrassment of forgetting his clients' names. They were *all* John - simple! Then, after the initial snipping was concluded, he would bring out the clippers. To top off the Freddie Fielding Special, the clippers, which were set to as short as they would go, were raked roughly up the back and sides of the sitter's head, almost to the crown, for that perfect coconut look. All that then remained was a liberal dollop of Brylcreem, and a deft back-flick with the comb, which left the unfortunate victim looking like either Stan Laurel or Hitler, depending on hair type. As the hairs were being vigorously brushed from the neck, Freddie would round off his performance with the time-honoured barber's mantra, 'Anything for the weekend, John?' whereupon money, and the occasional packet of what David presumed was chewing gum, would change hands.

Some sitters would ask to have their hair singed. This fascinated the young lad, because he could see no earthly reason why anyone in their right mind would purposely want their hair, albeit fleetingly, set on fire. Above Freddie's sink was a small water heater with an open pilot light. Next to this was a shelf where he kept the tools of his trade and a jar full of white tapers. When a hair singe was requested, he would reach for a taper, insert it into the heater to light the end and then deftly whiz it over the newly-cut hair, melting the ends to a kind of teardrop shape, and supposedly sealing the hair shaft. This ritual was widely believed to stop people from getting colds. The science was unsound, to say the least, but it *was* proven beyond doubt that it stopped people from getting girlfriends.

David always dreaded the visit to the barbers, as did every right-thinking child of his generation. This was an era when a haircut was on par with the joy one got from a tetanus injection or a dental filling, and not the luxurious and pleasurable event it would one day become. This time, he was dreading it more than usual, because he was cultivating a new look which he rather liked, and he didn't want it tampered with. It was meant to echo the current thinking in Liverpool, but in reality it was nearer to pudding basin medieval. He rather optimistically believed that it made him resemble George Harrison, which socially speaking was a

20

vast improvement on his previous 'Young Hitler' look - the one he was about to be reunited with, once Freddie's current victim had been duly butchered and his ego brought down a peg or two.

New clients arrived as old ones shuffled off into the night with their temporary disfigurements, and finally David arrived at the head of the queue, quickly practising his lines for one last time before Freddie bolted on the booster seat and turned to indicate that the time had come. David hoisted himself up into the chair, cleared his throat and spoke:

"Mom said, could you leave it quite long on top with a fringe, and can you leave my sideburns on please? No Brylcreem and no singeing. Thank you."

Freddie had that look of a barber who had just heard some words, but had no intention of stringing them together to form a meaning. Compliance with the client's wishes was not an issue. They merely supplied the necessary funds for Freddie's vision, which was to devote a lifetime to mastering the short back and sides, uncluttered by thoughts of anything else. David could have asked for a curly perm or pigtails and the result would have been the same. He looked at himself in the mirror, and, heaving a sigh, gave way to the inevitable.

The last time he had visited the barber was prior to a family holiday in Weston Super Mare. On this occasion, Freddie had been more than usually liberal with the Brylcreem, and when David took a dip in the sea the coast guard hastily contacted the RSPB, who dropped everything and rushed over, just in case they were needed to clean up any Cormorants. Today's effort was well on track to be just as ghastly.

Five minutes later, the hair having been brushed conveniently down his neck (to avoid floor sweeping) and the gown removed, Freddie pocketed the payment and went into his spiel.

"I thank you John, here's your Cadbury's penny chocolate, and shall I cross you over the road?"

David thanked him for the chocolate and his offer, explaining that he wasn't going home that night, but to his grandparents' house, further up the hill. He intended to ask Freddie if he could possibly offer *him* something for the weekend, because he had taken rather a liking to the penny chocolates that were dished out to all the children - presumably as compensation for the awful hairstyles. However, asking for more chocolate for the weekend seemed a little too cheeky, and he hadn't the necessary funds if asked to pay, so he shelved the thought.

David left the little shop looking predictably like a young Brylcreemed and singed Adolf Hitler, and stared momentarily in disbelief at the dense pea-soup fog that had descended on Brierley Bank in the time it took to get a haircut. The yellow street lamps were glowing eerily through the pollution, and he was aware of the bristly hair beginning to stand up on the back of his neck as he slowly made his way up the high street.

David, as we have already established, had a very vivid imagination, and didn't much care for the dark at the best of times. Now, the fog seemed to make the darkness ten times scarier. In an attempt to lighten his mood, he screwed his eyes up and stared at the street lamps, twisting his head from side to side so that he could create interesting starburst effects. It was of no real use, spiritually speaking - he was still petrified. The problem was, he had recently been told a tale by one of his school friends about such a fog, which descended on a fishing village. This fog was home to hundreds of zombies, which had a rather disconcerting habit of popping into fishermen's cottages just as they were settling down to a nice Cornish pastie or fish pie, and scaring the living daylights out of them. David was now desperately trying to force these nasty images out of his head and encourage some nicer ones in. At least, he thought to himself, it was Friday, which gave him two days for his hair to be washed, restyled and to grow a little before school. It was traditional, upon sight of a freshly scalped child, for all and sundry to whack the back of the unfortunate pupil's head and shout 'Haircut!' at them, and the weekend's growth might just spare him this unpleasantness.

His attempts to reel in his imagination and think pleasant thoughts were not going too well, and before long his mind had returned to The Undead. An old man suddenly looming out of the fog at him without warning did nothing to steady his nerves. David's heart had temporarily deserted his ribcage and was bouncing around in his mouth, doing a particularly spirited Highland fling. Once more, every hair on the back of his newly-mown head stood to attention. The old man, who was merely walking home with his fish and chip supper, wished him 'goodnight', and carried on his way, oblivious to the trauma he had caused. As the timid schoolboy made his way up the hill, shadowy figures emerged without warning and disappearing seconds later into the gloom. A large dog behind an unseen gate, just inches away, let out a vicious growl that saw David only narrowly miss out on a new Olympic record for the Hop, Skip and Jump. His Y fronts, lovingly ironed and clean on that morning, only just managed to remain clean for the evening.

To take his mind off this latest trauma, David again tried to focus on nicer things, and remembered that he was calling in at Kettle's Toy Shop *en-route*. By his reckoning, he was just about level with the shop, but the fog was now so awful that he really couldn't tell for sure, and it was a skittish and jittery David Day that paused at the kerbside to get his bearings.

First, he would need to cross the road. There were no car noises, so he gingerly began to cross. Luckily, any car that was passing would be doing so at a snail's pace, unless the driver was intent on messy suicide. There were distant rumblings coming up the hill, but nothing sounded close enough to cause concern. He could now make out the welcoming lights of the toy shop window, and before long he was standing with his nose pressed against it, looking at a colourful array of toys, tricks, sweets and games. His mood lightened considerably when he realized that the shop was still open for business. He had good money to spend and needed some respite from the cold, frightening night.

It was a good indication of how unnerved David was by being in the fog that he saw a visit to Miss Kettle's as the preferred alternative. Ordinarily, he would be full of trepidation about entering her establishment. Physically, the woman was no oil painting, if one discounted the works of Hieronymus Bosch. She was the spitting image of the grandmother from the Giles cartoons, or maybe Ena Sharples from Coronation Street, but with even less charm. Miss Kettle would have had great trouble winning a beauty contest if the only other competitors were warthogs which had been banished from their neck of the woods for being too ugly.

Concentrating on the merely physical aspects of this lady might sound uncharitable, were it not for the fact that her personality was decidedly ugly too. It was surely one of life's best philosophical jokes that a person who had no charm, no sense of humour and certainly no love of children whatsoever, should be allowed to run the local toy and joke shop. The woman was a tyrant and a force to be reckoned with.

Once, when David's mother had been shopping in the high street, she had purchased sweets for him from the little old-fashioned sweet shop further down the road, and then visited Miss Kettle's to buy him an Airfix model tank kit for his birthday. Miss Kettle came out from the back room in curlers and regulation pinafore, and cast her unpleasant beady eyes over the young lady in her shop, noticing the small bag of sweets, which she also sold.

"If you choose to buy your sweets from somewhere else, you can bugger off there for all your other stuff as well. Good day to you," she growled, and presumably crawled back under her bridge at the back of the shop, to rejoin her Troll friends.

It was with not a little trepidation, therefore, that timid, well-mannered little David pushed open the door and walked over the creaking bare floorboards to the high counter, with an Airfix Sopwith Camel kit on his mind, and the money in his sticky little paw. He tinkled the bell, itself an act of foolhardy bravado. The ogre had provided a bell, but heaven help those who were brave enough to actually use it.

He waited a while, but Miss Kettle did not appear.

Taking his life into his hands, he tinkled the bell again, but still she did not appear. David walked over to the end of the counter, where the hinged top was raised and propped against the wall. He ventured through the gap, and shouted into the back room, but no one answered. Turning and looking behind the counter, he nearly jumped out of his own skin. For the third time in ten minutes, his neck hairs stood to attention, and his heart made another spirited dash for the exit.

Miss Kettle lay flat out and lifeless under the open and emptied till, with a huge red bump protruding from her white hair.

David stood rooted to the spot with fear. He tried to shout 'Help!', but the word just wouldn't form. He clutched at his groin as if desperate to go to the toilet (Just as he did five minutes before the end of his recent mock eleven-plus exam, when he couldn't work out how many buckets of water Jim and Jane needed to fill a hole six feet square by three feet deep). Then at last, his brain re-established contact with his legs, and he was out of the shop and back into the fog before you could say 'Dead Woman in a Toy Shop'.

Once outside, his main priority was to skedaddle as fast as he could to his grandparents' house. He was just about to put in some serious groundwork, when he heard voices in the fog just ahead of him. He toyed with the notion of telling the voices what he'd just seen and asking them to help him get home, but when voice number one spoke, David froze in his tracks. He could tell the owner of that voice anywhere.

"What did you have to hit the ugly bitch for? Now what bin we gunna do?"

The words were delivered slowly by a slow man, with a voice that was afflicted by an awful speech impediment. This wasn't the same kind of problem that David's friend Terry Deakin had. It sounded more like the owner of the voice had a large dollop of Vaseline in his throat, so that the word Bitch came out as 'Biksch'. The Elephant Man probably had the edge on him for clear diction, and certainly for intelligence.

A second voice answered in the darkness.

"She was putting up a fight, bitin' and scratchin', that's why! Fat lot of use yow were, you dozy cretin."

This second voice had what David recognized as a Birmingham accent. Outsiders would perhaps have failed to spot the difference, but the voice was more nasal than a Brierley Banker's, with 'bitin'' pronounced 'boitin''.

"Well," replied voice number one, "Nothing we can do about it now, Chinny. If I ends up paying for this, I'll bloody kill yer."

The voices began to trail off as the two men headed down the high street, straight past a terrified young boy hidden in an alleyway, still clutching his groin in a desperate attempt to prevent it from leaking. For the second time in as many minutes, his brain had refused to communicate with his legs, and was only now softening its resolve and agreeing to resume meaningful discussion. The debate concluded, and terms and conditions hammered out betwixt management and workforce, the legs threw themselves into the task like two demented pieces of knotted string, belting up the fogbound hill at a pace that Roger Bannister wouldn't have been ashamed of.

CHAPTER 4

Bertha and Reuben

At number fourteen, Thorns Avenue, Brierley Bank, Reuben Cole, a small wiry sixty-something in belt, braces, waistcoat and collarless shirt, was standing in front of a mirror in the tiny kitchen-cum-sitting room, combing and re-combing his heavily Brylcreemed three sprigs of hair. This gentle, quietly-spoken grandfather liked his hair just so, even if there was precious little of it. Bertha, his larger, jolly ex-barmaid wife of forty years, stared at him with a big grin on her ample, double-chinned face.

"Well, I've never known anybody spend so long combing so little."

At least, that is what the subtitles would have said. The older generation of Black Country folk, and especially those from Brierley Bank, spoke a dialect that was reputed to be the nearest thing to the original Anglo Saxon left in England. That said, a few miles down the road in The Lye, it was even more unfathomable.

Reuben smiled the smile of a quiet and loyal husband who had heard all the hair jokes a million times, and long since become immune. Here was a truly gentle soul, who liked his snooker and billiards, his boxing and horse racing, and the occasional pint of mild, a drink that was almost certainly named in his honour.

He was not an articulate or indeed an educated man. His whole life had been spent in the same small town, working for the same big steelworks. When he went out, he was always dapper and neat, with a three-piece suit and tie with tiepin, pearl cufflinks and fob watch. His gold wristwatch bore the inscription;

'Reuben Cole - For twenty-five years loyal service to Eliza Wellings and Co.'

He was going to give it to his grandson, David, when the lad was old enough to appreciate it.

They say that animals are good judges of character, and Reuben went a long way to proving this theory. He had a bond with creatures of all shapes and sizes that few could match. His pet cockatiel, Beaky, or Beak for short, would walk along his arm and lie down in the palm of his hand, waiting to be stroked. Once Reuben had worked his magic, the bird would appear to fall asleep and lie there contentedly for ages. Bad- tempered dogs that would think nothing of removing great chunks of flesh from the postman's leg rolled over and surrendered when Reuben started talking to them.

His was a life of simple pleasures. He pottered around in the garden, growing carrots and potatoes, stopping occasionally to chat to a passing robin and maybe coax it onto his hand with a worm. He woke each morning at six o'clock, because he loved the still peace at that time of day. He'd leave Bertha sleeping, and return with a cup of tea for her at seven.

Bertha, at first glance, was not a good physical match for Reuben. Larger, more robust and more gregarious, she had been for many years a barmaid in and around the Old Hill area, a few miles away. This had been a Methodist stronghold in Victorian times, with fire and brimstone preachers ranting on about the evils of drink to a bunch of nailmakers that worked in furnaces all day long, and drank twenty pints each lunchtime, just to cool them off a bit. Because of this biblical heritage, the local accent was heavily laced with thees, thys and thines. When friends passed in the street, they would often ask, 'How bist thee?' curiously employing a derivation of the German verb 'to be'.

Bertha would often be helped up onto one of the bigger square cast-iron pub tables towards the end of the evening, to give them a spirited rendition of 'Ramona', or 'Are You Lonesome Tonight?' complete with spoken recitation in the middle. Sometimes, when something amused her, she would laugh so heartily that she would cry and become utterly helpless. Her daughter Ruby and her grandson David were similarly afflicted. Ruby had been known to become totally convulsed with laughter over seemingly insignificant things, such as, for example, the way pied wagtails walked in a jaunty, comical fashion, rather than hopped. Watching a comedy film in the local fleapit cinema, she would always get the joke at least five minutes after everyone else had laughed and moved on, and begin to shriek uncontrollably, like someone had triggered a fire alarm, much to the embarrassment of Leonard, her loyal husband.

Bertha, when not singing ballads on a table with a couple of sherries swilling around inside her, was often to be found loading up the cooking pot with pig's feet and assorted lentils, or making faggots and mushy peas. Presently, she was having a quick breather prior to preparing the evening meal, and indulging in a little tonsorial banter at the old chap's expense.

"Our David's late tonight, Reuben," she observed, looking at her wall clock. "Do you think he's alright? The fog's gone terrible."

"I'll have a walk down the road and get the evening paper," suggested Reuben, concerned. "I'll see if I can see him," and with a final adjustment to his three sprigs, he pulled on his overcoat and flat cap, and set off.

Two minutes later, man and boy were back in the fold, boy looking perished but more than a little relieved to be in a cosy environment once more.

"You look like one that's eaten and thrown up!" said Bertha, rubbing his face briskly to get some colour back into it. Her expressions were always wonderfully expressive. "What on earth's up with thee?"

David longed to tell her the horror story that he had witnessed only ten minutes previously, but something prevented him. His usually quick mind was in turmoil, but he knew somewhere in the chaos was a goodish reason to not reveal all. He just needed a little time to think it through.

"Oh, there's nothing up with me, Gran. I was just a bit frightened 'cause of the fog, and I couldn't work out where I was."

"Well, sit down and read your comic, I've nearly done the dinner. When's your mother coming?"

"She'll be here after breakfast tomorrow. Erm, can I sleep in your bed tonight, Gran?"

"Course you can!" smiled Bertha, putting her sizeable arms around the lad. "Granddad will sleep in the spare room, won't you, Reuben? He prefers it anyway because he says my snoring's terrible. Mind you, it can't be any worse than his blowing off."

David smiled for the first time since he arrived. "It must be your faggots, Gran."

After dinner, David played cards and dominoes with his granddad until the old man decided to slip down the road to the Blue Ball pub for a quick half of mild with his next-door neighbour, Wes. Then he amused himself by drawing dinosaurs with his new thirteen-colour biro, in one of the many sketchbooks that his family provided to keep him quiet.

That night he lay next to his grandmother in bed, unable to drop off because of a sound in his right ear akin to a trained truffle-hunting pig unearthing treasures on a Tuscan hillside. He kept seeing the same, vivid image of Mrs Kettle lying dead on her shop floor, which unnerved him, having never seen a dead person before. He hoped she was just hibernating, like his hamster, and she'd get up when the heating came on, but he knew in his heart of hearts that this was unlikely. He'd deliberately not told his grandparents about what he'd seen, because something at the back of his mind had warned him that there were complications. Now, with time on his hands to reflect, he saw more clearly what they were.

The voice with the awful speech impediment was Herbert Rhys - the surname was pronounced 'Reece', to rhyme with grease. This slow-witted, stick-thin village idiot of some twenty summers was none other than the son of Charlie Rhys - better know as Sergeant Rhys - the beat bobby with the sole responsibility for keeping the residents of Brierley Bank on the straight and narrow. He was an amiable but tough middle-aged copper who patrolled this small town on a bicycle, and stood no messing. Many a young lad had been clipped round the ear for various crimes ranging from scrumping apples to knocking on doors and running off. Serious offences all, and once Charlie had passed on this information to the respective parents, the miscreants could fully expect to get their backsides dusted all over again when they got home. Charlie was just one large bloke on an old bike, but he knew everything, and everyone. How could David possibly tell Charlie that his own son had robbed and murdered an old lady, with his evil accomplice, Chinny? 'Charlie the Police Officer' would hand his dim-witted offspring over to the authorities, but then again, 'Charlie the Dad' would surely cover up this horrendous act to the best of his ability. Blood, as David had heard Mr Perriman say in assembly, is thicker than water. And what if Charlie decided to deflect his fellow officers from the truth? Put them off the scent. It was conceivable that he would lie through his teeth to protect his own son, stupid as the lad was. Maybe he'd even accuse David of being the murderer. He'd stand up in court and point at the trembling eleven-year-old in the dock.

"Yes, your Honour. That was the boy what I saw clubbing the old dear with a blunt instrument, and making off with a Sopwith Camel Airfix Kit."

No, this policeman could not be told what David had seen, and, just for the moment, neither could David's family. This needed time for contemplation. Perhaps he could discuss it with Mally Lobes. They were best friends, and he trusted him. Between them, they could formulate a plan, just like Jennings and Darbishire (The characters from his favourite books, not the hamsters he named in their honour). They always outsmarted the criminals with cunning wheezes and saved the day. The problem was, Jennings and Darbishire usually just solved minor mysteries, like who stole the rugger cup from the dormitory. This was a bit more serious. This was a rea- life murder.

David's eyelids finally began to droop, and he could fight sleep no longer. He turned over, put his arm around his grandmother's ample and comforting waist, and was gone.

CHAPTER 5

Brierley Bank

Reuben was not one for vegetating in bed. Time spent asleep was time wasted, in his opinion. Not for him 'those slices of death', as it was once so eloquently, if a little morbidly, put. The only trouble with his otherwise admirable philosophy was that he did tend to rope those close to him into sharing it. David, for example, quite liked his shut-eye, and regarded any winks over and above the regulation forty as a good thing, and to be encouraged. Growing lads needed rest, not a cup of hot steaming tea in the middle of the night. To make matters worse, he was just in the middle of a particularly fine dream, and after a twilight tea party, who could guarantee that he'd pick up where he'd left off, (with Mandy from 3c, for those intrigued by the sordid details) and not plunge into some horrible encounter with cadaverous toy shop owners, or murderous criminals in creepy fogs?

He paid lip service to his tea and promptly sank back into a deep sleep, from which he groaningly and stretchingly emerged at nine. The first few minutes of consciousness were very pleasant, as he explored ways of filling the brand new day. If the weather was fine, he'd attempt to reconstruct his bike. If it wasn't so good, he'd curl up by the fire with his Sopwith Camel.

David was far too impatient to read instructions, so most of the models hanging from his ceiling on cotton threads had wings glued on back to front and decals in all the wrong places. He was, like his dad, a perfectionist, but there are two types of perfectionist. His dad was organized, and every tool had to be laid out, ready for use. The instructions were read and re-read, and any little potentially tricky sections were sorted out in advance. The man had the patience of a saint - unlike David, who rushed at things like a bull at a gate. He *presumed* he understood things, and realized all too late that he didn't. He squirted glue liberally to the wrong areas, which were then plainly visible on the finished model. The decals would be floated in a saucer of water, and in his haste to apply them they would be stuck together or torn beyond repair. He never read the part that suggested he should paint a section before assembly, until *after* assembly. David was, despite his prowess with a pencil and paints, a complete disaster at model making. Only after the mad impulsive rush of blood to the head was over did he suddenly become The Perfectionist. Then the artistic temperament would come into play, and he became full of self-loathing and disgust because, as usual, he had rushed into things. The wild promises to himself to 'take my time next time' had again been ignored. It was then but a short trip to the tantrum and the ceremonial hurling of the craft project into the nearest pedal bin.

And then the thought hit him, like a sizeable cobble to the back of the head from a wayward catapult. He didn't *have* a Sopwith Camel. A small matter of dead Miss Kettles with lumps on their heads had put the kybosh on that.

The hope that all this had been a bad dream had been dashed. It *had* happened, and, as yet, he'd done nothing about it. He was sure the two men hadn't seen him, so he didn't feel personally threatened, but it was his duty to bring these two villains to justice. He didn't like Miss Kettle much, but he wouldn't wish her fate on anyone. A nasty bump on the head maybe, but not murder!

David quickly jumped out of bed and put on the neatly-folded school clothes he had abandoned in a heap on the bedroom floor the previous night. Those lesser-known characters from folklore, the Clothes-Folding Faeries, had been doing their rounds whilst the young lad slept, and now the young master offered them his pyjamas to work on. Once dressed, he wandered into the tiny sitting room and greeted his grandparents. David usually ate a hearty breakfast when staying with them, which was strange, because at home he barely touched a thing until lunchtime. This Saturday morning, however, he was off his food, which prompted Bertha to ask if he was feeling unwell. He replied that everything was fine, and whiled away the time till his mother arrived trying to teach the cockatiel to talk.

David often stayed for the weekend, which was enjoyable for him, because he loved his grandparents and the change of scenery. It was also convenient for his mom and dad, because they could do little jobs around the house. More importantly, it gave them a bit of time to have a lie in, and see what developed.

It was, as a consequence of this arrangement, a flushed and slightly bedraggled Ruby Day that came to pick David up, half an hour later. Shyly, she put it down to the gusty November winds, whistling up Brierley Bank High Street. This particular weekend, David was going home on

Saturday, because he wanted to go to a Speedway meeting that evening in nearby Cradley Heath. The Heathens were competing against Wolverhampton Wolves, and there were always fireworks when these keen local rivals met.

Much as he loved his grandparents, David wasn't really as keen on spending entire Sundays there. He'd climb downstairs on Sunday mornings to be met by some depressing religious radio programme or other, which would set the tone for the whole day. Bertha and Reuben didn't have a television, so the radio was on all day long, and when the songs of praise dirge had concluded, the Sunday dinner preparations would commence. Bertha peeled and chopped things, accompanied by Two-Way Family Favourites, which, to David, even made the church programme sound cheerful, with its requests for maudlin ballads and country and western music, dedicated to soldiers from somewhere called BFPO something-or-other in Luxemburg - wherever that was. Elvis would croon, "Are you Lonesome Tonight?" and Bertha would provide the harmonies as she peeled the spuds. The all-pervading smell of Johnson's Furniture Wax and the clatter of the Ewbank sweeper would only add to the gloom.

Often, to keep him quiet, Bertha would ask David to pop the pea pods and empty the contents into a colander. He quite liked doing this, because the peas tasted sweet, and he would consume vast quantities, often leaving none for the dinner. Also, the pods were quite interesting things in their own right, and they formed the basis of many a game. The mind of a child is a wondrous thing. It can make a game out of anything, and this talent is sadly lost forever when the child becomes an adult. David was equally entranced with his piggy bank full of threepenny bits, which became soldiers or building blocks, depending on his mood, and amused him for hours after Sunday dinner - or lunch, as the southerners would have everyone call it.

The radio was at its best around dinner time, with Round the Horn, Billy Cotton's Band Show, and Jimmy Clitheroe. David quite liked the comedy programmes, especially the Goon Show, which appealed to his abstract sense of humour. Here were sown the first seeds of youthful rebellion, as he argued the case for Milligan and Co. against a grandmother who reckoned they were all 'too bloody daft to laugh at.'

Usually, he and his mother would be donning overcoats at teatime and saying their farewells to the soundtrack of 'Sing Something Simple', with the Mike Sammes Singers, a programme so maudlin that it almost certainly prompted them to head home. The whole programme consisted of a dreary bunch of singers drearily singing a dreary bunch of songs. To this eleven-year-old boy, the new sound of the Beatles was like an invigorating blast of fresh air, blowing away the musty, furniture polish and Sunday dinner-tainted croonings of the older generation.

Mercifully, on this occasion, David had been spared the Sunday ritual, and after a quick cup of tea, mother and child went out through the front door, waving fond goodbyes until the following weekend, mother with home-grown carrots and child with Cadbury's penny chocolates and some extra pocket money. As they walked down to where the high street began, David's mind was in overdrive, wondering what he would see when he got to the scene of the crime.

Brierley Bank was the epicentre of the Black Country; a unique area just a few miles from Birmingham, but as different as fresh Parmesan to the foul-smelling toenail cheese they sell in small tubs. Not that anyone from Brierley

Bank had heard of Parmesan. The choice offered in nineteen-sixty-five, in any of the many greengrocers' shops, consisted of 'sharp' or 'mild'. That was pretty much it.

The town was more or less one long street built on a rather steep hill. Just past the top end there were open-cast mines, with pit heads that stood dramatically against some of the best sunsets to be found anywhere. The town itself appeared at first to be made up entirely of butcher's shops and public houses, which hinted to the astute observer what kind of folk lived there. A second glance would reveal a variety of other shops, mainly small family-run businesses, with old wood-panelled interiors. There was a wool shop, so that mothers could knit embarrassing Fair Isle jumpers that never fitted their offspring. They also knitted balaclavas and gloves, and they would have knitted shoes if they could have done. It is heartening to record that no children from the area ever grew up to become armed robbers or terrorists, which suggested that their mothers had raised them properly. A cynic, however, would argue that it was more likely to be because their offspring had virtually all suffered from balaclava abuse as children, and couldn't stomach the thought of wearing them ever again in adult life.

An old-fashioned hardware store supplied the good people of the town with gas mantles, mousetraps and paraffin lamps, nails, screws and firelighters. The coal merchant next door delivered sacks of coal to the house, and billowing smoke from thousands of chimneys every teatime ensured that there would be many more pea-soup fogs like the one they had witnessed on Friday night.

They passed Cedric's Café, or Ced's Caff, as it was known, and if Brierley Bank was the epicentre of the Black Country, then this café was the epicentre of Brierley Bank. The owner, who coincidentally had the same name as his café, was what is known in more polite circles as 'a character', though customers who had seen him poke his fat, tobacco-stained finger into their coffee in order to ascertain how long they'd been making it last them, probably had their own name for him. Boswell and Dr Johnson would certainly have turned their noses up at the place, but there were plenty of people for whom good food, intellectual conversation and polite society were not an issue, that regularly patronized the place to idle away an hour until the bus arrived.

Mrs and Master Day were fast approaching the toy shop now, and David's heart was once more doing a fair impression of a Mexican jumping bean. Just the Chemist's shop and the off licence to pass and they were there. David asked his mother if they could stop off to get his Sopwith Camel, explaining that he'd not bothered to get it when the fog became thicker, but once again he was thwarted. Miss Kettle's shop was closed. Ruby tried the door again, in case it was just a little stiff, but, no, it was definitely locked.

"That's strange!" she said. "I would have thought she would have been open today. Saturday is her busiest day."

They looked in the window for a note or a sign of life, but there was nothing. It took all of David's resolve not to blurt out the story or give the game away in some way, but he held himself together.

"Perhaps she's just not well, and decided to have a day off," he suggested.

"Maybe, but I've known her for years, and the miserable old thing's never been ill once in all that time, that I can remember," she mused. "Oh well! You'll have to call in another day."

As they turned away from the window, David's face drained of colour as he saw Herbert Rhys and a man that he did not recognize, carrying a large, coffin-sized plywood box out of the entry next door. They were puffing and panting as they got to the rusty and decrepit white van parked near to where David and his mother stood. David stared with horror as they struggled to load the box into the vehicle. Herbert's accomplice was the first to speak.

"Well," he said conspiratorially to his dim colleague, "Another one bites the dust. We did well out of her, mate. Now let's clear off before we're found out."

David's facial expression modulated from horror to righteous indignation. He couldn't believe that they could be so callous about human life, even if it was Miss Kettle's, and have the gall to chat openly about her demise in the high street.

It is often the case that such brazen, criminal types are quite open about discussing their activities in public, because they believe that no one else is remotely interested in their business. This was a foolish habit if one lived in Brierley Bank, the town that invented and patented the two fat ladies gossiping over the garden fence. Everyone knew everyone else in this incestuous little town, which was both a blessing and a curse for those who inhabited the place.

Mother and child continued down the street; child glancing back every second or so, to the point where mother had to criticize what she thought was the child's obsession with 'blasted Sopwith Camels'. If only she knew. If only he could tell her, but now wasn't the time.

They were opposite the old cobbler's shop now, and were turning into the narrow alleyway that ran parallel to

Benjamin Bloomer's, the chainmakers. Through the broken windows high up in the wall, David could see the bright fire flashes and hear the ear-shattering bangs of hammer on metal. He shuddered at the thought of ever having to work there all day, just to make a living. All the men looked and sounded the same. Sweaty, dirty bodies with huge beer-bellies and voices like the fog horn on the Titanic, which was rather apt, as the chain made at Bloomers was actually used on the ship, and the huge anchors were made just down the road. Proud heritage and honest toil were all very well, but even at eleven, David knew he wanted no part of it. He'd seen his beloved dad come home, filthy and tired from making his wonderfully accurate machine tools from chunks of solid metal, and it didn't appeal.

"Accurate to a thou., David," he'd say proudly, to a little boy who hadn't the foggiest idea what a thou. (a thousandth of an inch) was, and probably wouldn't care until his dad wasn't there any more to say it.

Something was troubling him as they walked together through the noisy alley. The two callous robbers had done their dirty deed, and he shuddered to think what was in the huge, coffin-shaped box. Had they returned to cart her off, lock up the shop and turn off the lights? It certainly wasn't done at the time, because he had been in the shop himself, and seen her body. He'd heard them talking and presumed they had walked off into the fog. Had they gone back to the shop later that evening, after he was safely ensconced at his grandparents' house, or maybe covered their tracks on Saturday morning? Either way, the door was now locked, and it was only a matter of time before people became suspicious and the police were called.

Surely then, he could just forget all about this unpleasantness, and let nature take its course. Sergeant Rhys would be summoned, and he would set the wheels in motion, with the forensic boys dusting everywhere, and dragnets cast. David need not get involved. Interpol would naturally be informed, and no doubt the dim-wit and the Brummie would be arrested trying to catch the ferry to the Isle of Wight. Justice would be done; all David needed to do was sit back with a good Airfix model and a cup of tea and await results. The police weren't too bright, but Herbert was a lot dimmer than they were, so it shouldn't take them long.

These were the arguments being put forth by the little demon sitting on David's left shoulder. Now the little angel on his right shoulder gave tongue.

"It is your *duty* to get involved, David," it whispered to him, through the itchy wool of his new balaclava. "You are an honest and conscientious boy. You can't sit back and ignore this. A woman has been killed, and *you* know who did it. You can't let the native hue of resolution be sicklied o'er by the pale cast of thought. If t'were done when t'is done, t'is best t'were done quickly!"

David didn't quite understand the actual detail of what the little angel was saying, but he did get the gist, and was impressed by how poetically she'd put it. Furthermore, he knew in his heart of hearts that she was right, and so, in the few minutes it took to walk to their home, he had formulated a plan.

CHAPTER 6

A Comedy of Errors

After a quick cheese sandwich accompanied by the obligatory Heinz tomato soup, David tried to put his cycle speedway bike back together on the back yard. Typically, he had deconstructed the machine in his usual frenzied fashion, forgetting to make notes, mental or otherwise, on how it all went back together. There seemed to be far more bits than the bike needed, so he simply left out the ones that looked unnecessary. This gave the thing a fairly satisfactory appearance if viewed from a distance, but when he attempted to wheel it back into the shed, it emitted a noise similar to that of two building bricks being ground together forcibly, with a feral cat trapped between them. Both front and back wheels instantly seized and several nuts sheared off, ricocheting across the garden like machine gun bullets.

At this juncture, David suddenly turned upon himself with a violent spasm of unintelligible self-loathing, threw the crippled machine across the yard and kicked the various bits that had been surplus to requirements in a number of directions. His dad emerged from the garage after a hard day's metal-filing, just in time to see yet another mongrel bike meet its maker.

"One day, you'll learn to organize yourself before you start messing, or better still, just let me do it for you," he said, knowing full well that he had been exactly the same as a boy, and nothing any adult said would make one iota of difference. "Anyway, forget that for now. Come in the house. I've got something for you."

This fairly innocuous statement, oft heard on a Saturday lunchtime as his dad arrived home from work, always set David's pulse racing. He dashed indoors, eager to see what he'd brought home this time.

Leonard Day loved to bring home surprises. Given that he left the house early, six days a week, and ended up at the same factory a few miles away, from which he duly returned, like clockwork, at tea time each evening, it was quite remarkable how he frequently managed to bring home some interesting piece or other. David never questioned how this could be. It was just something his dad did, and he loved it. One day he would emerge from the garage with a zither, the next a periscope. Saturday could produce a German helmet, and Wednesday a Victorian picture book. They never knew what he'd turn up with next.

It was David's role to 'improve' these treasures, thus ensuring that they did not increase in value in the years to come. His poor, ever-patient dad had often begged him to look after the various items he presented him with, because some were antiques, and probably worth a lot of money. Whilst David agreed in principle, he thought that some renovation was often called for to realize the true potential of the items. Thus, the old saxophone got painted a fetching shade of blue, whilst the zither - well over a hundred years old, was varnished and then left outside on the lawn one winter's night, which meant Arthur Negus had one less thing to worry about. The periscope, reportedly from a Nazi U Boat, was left at school overnight and duly vanished. The microscope was swapped for an injury-stricken Manchester City Subbuteo set, with a boy who, it turned out, had left to live in Wales. A rather fetching piece of amateur calligraphy put paid to the rare first edition of A.A. Milne's Winnie the Pooh, and the very collectable Edwardian shock therapy machine, which was widely believed to be good for the nerves, was quietly disposed of by Ruby Day, once she had fully regained consciousness.

It was, therefore, with great enthusiasm and anticipation that David stood in the kitchen, waiting for his dad to unveil the latest item for the collection. Len carefully opened the plastic Woolworth's carrier bag, and took out a small cardboard box with holes punched in the top and sides. He set it down on the kitchen table and opened the lid with caution.

"Come and have a look!" he said, gesturing to David to get closer.

Inside the box, partially covered by shredded pink paper, was a small and very timid new hamster.

"Darbishire!" exclaimed David, with a huge grin on his face. "I thought you were bringing me another of your World War Two thingies!"

"Well, I hope this wasn't a disappointment then. And talking of interesting thingies, I might have a few more coming next week, if my mate from the steel firm turns up. I've got first refusal."

Ruby's eyes turned heavenwards, in that exasperated, 'boys and their toys, when will they ever grow up' kind of way, and carried on knitting her vacuum-cleaner cover.

David dashed off to the shed to get Jennings's old cage. It was looking a little the worse for wear, and smelling to high heaven, so he put it down on some unread newspapers and proceeded to clean it up prior to introducing the new arrival. When it was ready and stocked with fresh food and water, he carefully got hold of Darbishire, placing him in his new home. It sniffed around for a minute or two, exploring its new surroundings, and then, like a small and furry Greta Garbo, decided that it 'vonted to be alone' and headed for its sleeping quarters, where it steadfastly remained.

The excitement now over, Darbishire was returned to the shed and allowed to acclimatise in peace. Ruby reminded her husband that they had promised to pop over to the caravan at the weekend, just to make sure it was tidy and secure for the winter, so someone would have to look after the new arrival. To this end, she went out onto the back yard, tapped the fence and called 'Glad!' as loudly as was considered ladylike. A few seconds later, a large jolly woman came out, with the remnants of some foodstuff still tumbling around in her mouth. Ruby had long since given up on apologizing for interrupting Gladys's meals, because, as far as she could make out, the woman was constantly grazing, and the likelihood of speaking to a Gladys *without* a mouthful of the stuff was remote.

It is sometimes useful, when trying to create a quick pen portrait, to describe a character's physical appearance by comparing them to someone in the public eye; hence Miss Kettle was described earlier as the double of the Giles grandma. This technique can be employed to good effect once more, because Gladys was - as near as 'damn it' is to swearing - Hattie Jacques. The resemblance was even more uncanny because Glad was kitted out in a midwife's uniform, which made her look as if she were grabbing a quick snack in-between takes on the set of the latest Carry On film.

"Hello Rube!" she spluttered, through a pound or two of home-made sponge cake, sending crumbs flying in every direction.

"Hello Glad," replied Rube. "Could you possibly do us a big favour and feed David's new hamster next weekend, while we're away down the caravan? You just have to change the water and see that it's stocked up with seeds - nothing too awful!"

"Course, Rube," said Glad, who was still having trouble with her problematic cake, like a boa constrictor that had taken on a larger than average capybara and was regretting ever getting involved. "but I'll let Frank deal with it, if you don't mind. I'm a bit squeamish with rodents."

"So am I," agreed Ruby, shuddering theatrically, "but I thought, after what you do all day, delivering babies, a small hamster wouldn't worry you."

"Yes, funny that. We women go through so much pain, blood and gore, and we leap onto the nearest chair and scream when a cute little mouse scurries by!"

She turned to David. "And it doesn't seem ten minutes since I delivered this one here, and now look at him. He's as tall as you already Rube, and he's only eleven, *and* he had the hardest head I've ever come across, bless him! I was stitching your poor mother for an hour after she'd pushed your head through."

She rubbed her hand through David's Hitler hairdo. He hated it when grown ups did that, the way Italian kids must hate having their cheeks pinched.

"You don't know what we mothers go through to give birth to you lot. And they grow up too fast, Rube. It's David's last year at school, and I don't know where the time's gone."

Ruby, who was a sentimental soul, looked at her son fondly and hugged him, much to his embarrassment. She made all the necessary arrangements for Frank's access to the shed and thanked her neighbour profusely. Gladys made her excuses and tootled back to the kitchen to get on the outside of another slab of sponge cake.

With Darbishire settled in, and catching up on some overdue shut-eye, David turned his attention to the Speedway meeting, and more importantly, his liaison with Mally to discuss the Kettle affair. He wolfed down his fish fingers, peas and chips and swallowed a quick cup of tea, before dashing upstairs to change. He put on his warm jumper, bobble hat and Cradley scarf in corporate green and white, and grabbed his lucky thirteen-colour biro and clipboard from under the bed. These last two items were essential for filling in the programme at the race meeting, and David's board was especially fine, as it had a small battery-operated light attached to the top, so that he could see when all the track lights dimmed. His dad had spent ages in the shed, constructing it in typical perfectionist fashion, and reluctantly allowed his son to 'improve' it with his artistic skills. The result was a beautiful action painting of a bike broadsiding around the track, executed in Humbrol enamels. True to form however, David had been too impatient to let the colours dry properly, and the first programme to be clipped onto the board had stuck solidly to the paint, ruining hours of work by father and son alike.

"Patience is a virtue, son," explained his weary dad, on seeing the latest in a long line of disasters.

"Yes, dad, but so is impatience, sometimes!" said a little boy who was often too clever for his own good. "At least it gets things done!"

The doorknocker clattered a few times, and the two-tone voice from without screamed, "DAY-*VID!*"

When Black Country lads called for each other, they literally did just that - they shouted the name of the person they had come to see, rather than knock the door. David rushed to the old outhouse to greet his school friend, who was similarly clad in green and white scarf. He said goodbye to his parents, who in turn warned the two of them to behave, not talk to strangers and come straight back home, preferably with a group of people they knew. They repeated their message to make sure their daydreaming young innocent had heard them, and heard them well. A few months before, they may not have felt the need to reinforce their words in this way, but that was before Hindley and Brady.

Now the world had changed, and it could never go back.

The two friends walked off down the front steps, thrilling to the distant sounds of music and commentary from elderly loudspeakers in a stadium two miles away. As they passed the houses on the estate, one by one, doors would open, and more people in their green and white livery would join the happy throng. Before long, the road to Cradley Heath Speedway resembled a scene from The Pied Piper of Hamelin. As they walked amongst this merry band, David began to unfold his tale to Mally, who was, literally, all ears.

Malcolm was one of those boys who could only be truly contented if he was blowing the remains of an unlucky bird-to-be out of an egg, or climbing a tree. He was a frustrated country boy living in a housing estate. To satisfy his cravings, he collected the cards that came free with Typhoo Tea, which featured freshwater fish, birds and assorted creatures of the forest. He knew the name of every butterfly in the British Isles, and had most of them impaled on pins in his bedroom. In short, he was perfectly capable, thank you very much, of teaching his grandmother how to suck eggs, and for that matter, how to stuff and mount a kestrel. A keen amateur taxidermist, he would often delight his parents by bringing home road-kill squirrels, and insist on preserving them in the fridge, next to the Robinson's Marmalade. Still at the beginning of his learning curve with this delicate and exacting art, sometimes the results were a little eccentric, and certainly lacking in symmetry. He was, after all, only eleven, and it would appear mean-spirited to be too critical.

"Mal," whispered David, with a sense of gravitas and secrecy reminiscent of Guido Fawkes as he addressed his co-conspirators, "I've got something really important to tell you, but you have to swear an oath not to say a word."

"Okay!" replied Mally, his beady eyes darting around suspiciously, as if in search of some hidden paparazzo with a zoom lens. "I swear on my birds' egg collection."

"That'll do," said David, well impressed. He knew what his egg collection meant to him. "Listen, I've witnessed a real-life murder."

He whispered this last word so quietly, to avoid the attentions of a couple of passing speedway fans, that Mally, even with his equipment, was struggling to hear.

"A murder?" hissed Mally. "Are you joking?"

"I wish it was a joke but it's real, and I'm scared to death!" hissed David, unwittingly clutching his groin as he spoke, as

52

he always did when he was panicking. Mally could see by his friend's rather unfortunate body language that this was serious. He huddled up close to David, as they walked over the patch of undeveloped land that was used as a shortcut to the stadium. If he had possessed a cloak and dagger, he would have employed them.

"Tell me all about it then," he said, and David did, keen to offload the turmoil that was wreaking untold havoc inside his head, and give poor Mally a bit of it, free of charge.

"What on earth are you going to do, Dave?" he asked, once the gruesome details had sunk in. "You've got to tell the Police!"

"Well, I can't tell Sergeant Rhys, can I? He'll just cover up the evidence 'cause it's his son. The pair of 'em might get me, and murder *me*."

"Grown ups don't murder kids, Dave," Mally assured him.

"They can now," David assured him. "Haven't you seen the newspapers? Anyway, I don't want to tell him. We'll have to think of another plan. We could lead the two men into a trap, like in my Jennings books. We could lay an ambush."

"I don't think so. Men are big, and they can fight kids easy. We'd need guns, or a rocket launcher or something or...." Mally paused, his lips pursed and his right index finger wagging knowingly, "or.... we could contact Scotland Yard"

"Brilliant," agreed David, impressed. "Scotland Yard are in charge of all the policemen in the country aren't they? They could investigate the murder for us. Bloomin' Rhys won't even know about it. We'll go straight to his bosses."

"Yeah, they might even arrest Sergeant Rhys as well, if he tries anything."

"I call him Sergeant Grease sometimes!" said David, convulsing with laughter.

"My dad calls him Rhys Pudding," chortled Mally, not to be outdone.

Their childish laughter was therapeutic, and eased the feeling of apprehension they were both experiencing. The first rule of combat was to mock the enemy. It helped a great deal in the struggle against Hitler, after all.

The corrugated green gates of the stadium beckoned, along with the wonderful and distinctive smell of the fuel, known as dope, which powered the speedway machines. The first bikes were going through their practice laps inside, the thrilling engine noises tearing into the cold night air. For now, all talk of murder and intrigue was suspended, and the two friends rattled through the turnstiles and purchased their programmes. Five thousand or more dedicated thrill seekers, collars turned against the bitter autumnal winds, cheered as one when the first four gladiators roared out onto the track. The boys allowed themselves a night of simple pleasure and a hotdog or two, with all conversation restricted to the racing. In the back of their minds, however, both knew that in the morning the earnest work would begin, and neither could shirk their responsibilities. They owed that much to Miss Kettle, even if they didn't particularly like her.

On Sunday morning, the friends agreed to meet at Mally's house, as soon as possible after breakfast. Mally supplied the paper, pen and envelope from a set his parents had given him for his birthday. The writing paper was cream, with a picture of a lapwing in the top right corner, and the envelope was of similar design, but this time with the bird on the flap. If this didn't tempt the head of Scotland Yard to hotfoot it over to the Midlands, nothing would. David, for his part, supplied the stamp, which he had borrowed from his mother's biscuit tin in the kitchen. They retired to the privacy of Mally's bedroom, which was full to the rafters with deranged-looking stuffed owls and squirrels mounted onto driftwood. Their uneven eyes peered down malevolently at the two boys as they began to compose their letter. David sat at Mally's desk, he having the neater handwriting of the two.

"Dear Sir," he began, looking for approval from his co-author.

"Put Dear Colonel," suggested Mally. "We'll write it to the boss of Scotland Yard."

"Okay! Dear Colonel," agreed David, bowing to Mally's superior knowledge in these matters. "My name is David Day, and I live at 3, Mary Road, Brierley Bank, Staffs. When I was going to my granny's, I found a dead lady in a shop called Miss Kettle's."

"Good so far," said Mally.

"She had been killed and her money was gone from the till because I looked."

Mally could not suggest any improvements at this stage.

"I was scared, so I hid in some fog. I heard two men talking about killing the lady. It was Herbert Rhys I know because he has got a funny voice. They put her in a coffin. Can you come to Brierley Bank and arrest them please?"

"That's it," said Mally, impressed with his colleague's succinctness. Eleven-year-olds believed firmly that brevity was the soul of wit, as Mr Lewis would often confirm when marking their scant essays.

"I'll just finish it off then," said David. "I think you can put 'Sincerely' or 'Unfaithfully', but I can never remember which one's right."

"You could put 'Love, David'. That's what my mom always puts," suggested Mally.

"Why does you mom put 'Love David' when her name's Ethel?" queried David, puzzled. "Anyway, it just doesn't sound right, saying 'Love' to a Colonel."

"I think it might be 'Discreetly'", suggested Mally, none too convincingly.

They agreed to toss for it, arguing that, whichever one they used, the Colonel would still get the gist.

"Yours Unfaithfully, David Day," mouthed David, as his pen scratched away. "P.S. Don't tell Sergeant Rhys because his son is the murderer."

The boys seemed pleased with their joint effort, which was duly folded and slipped into the envelope. Then a rather large and unexpected snag threatened to scupper their plans.

"What's the address?" asked David, pen poised.

"Er...I don't know," replied Mally, deflated. His serious face suddenly lightened. "But it's a very famous place. Everybody knows where to find it. My mom says that sometimes you can put just one or two words on an envelope and it still gets there, because the postmen are sort of detectives. Just put 'Scotland Yard, Scotland, England' on it, and it'll be okay."

And that is exactly what they did.

CHAPTER 7

The Caravan

Mr Lewis breezed into class with a cheerful 'Good morning, children', and began calling the register. When this daily chore was completed, he asked if anyone had lost a dog, or knew anyone locally who had done so, as he had acquired one at the weekend. He had been taking a bit of exercise over Brierley Bank Park at the time, for he was a firm believer in healthy bodies begetting healthy minds, and lived twenty-four hours per day in a blue tracksuit and white pumps. This dog, which he readily admitted would find it hard to win a beauty contest, was, nevertheless, a friendly, grateful, if timid creature that he had rather taken a shine to. Looks weren't everything, he told the attentive class, but this poor creature looked like one of young Malcolm's early taxidermy attempts. Realizing that the class were sniggering, and Malcolm had begun to look a little flushed, he moved swiftly on.

One got the impression that Mr Lewis rather liked this dumb animal, (the dog, not Malcolm) and wouldn't have been too concerned if the rightful owner was never found. It had come running over to him as he jogged, and at first he feared for his life, the creature being built roughly on the lines of Joe Louis.

Thankfully, however, it only sought friendship, and somehow it seemed to the kindly Welshman that it had seen precious little of that, as of even date. He couldn't be sure, of course, but sometimes one just had an intuition. The dog had appeared worn out and hungry and it had no collar, so Mr Lewis had taken it home, bathed it and fed it, and even as he spoke, the thing was languishing contentedly on his best chesterfield, no doubt thinking to itself, "This is far better than I've been used to!"

"I'll place a few notices around the shops and mention it in tomorrow's assembly, but in the meantime, I'll keep him with me."

A small hand shot up with some urgency. It was owned by Helen Cartwright.

"Sir, what have you called your dog, sir?"

"Well, Helen, I shouldn't really be calling the dog anything, or getting too attached, because it's probably got an owner somewhere who's desperate to get it back. I must admit though, I'd been calling it William, after my hero, William Shakespeare, but then I realized that it was a bitch! I can't really call it Willy now, can I?"

"Especially 'cause it hasn't got one, sir!" piped up Larry Homer, who set the whole class giggling behind their hands.

"No Larry, thank you. No, I'll have to call her Lady, after Lady Macbeth."

And, having concluded the 'Lost Dog' feature, he began handing out the exercise books that he had been marking over the weekend.

"Good work and neatly written, David," he said, as the book flew across the desk. "But why it says 'HAMSTER

RESURRECTION, TORNADO, FLOOD' and a load of other random statements on the back cover is still a mystery to me. I'm sure you have a ready explanation, but I'm almost tempted not to ask."

The other pupils began sniggering again, a habit which David was finding a touch too frequent for his tastes. He waited for the commotion to die down, and added the words FOG and MURDER to the list, his left hand cupped around his writing, as if he were in an exam, and the lad next to him was trying to copy.

At playtime, Mally confirmed that he had posted the letter, and all they had to do now was wait. They estimated that, because it was posted on a Sunday, it wouldn't be collected till Monday, which meant that Scotland Yard would hopefully receive it around Tuesday or Wednesday. Due to the enormity of the accusation enclosed therein, the police would surely be swarming all over the town by, say, Thursday, arresting suspects, spreading dragnets and contacting Interpol. With a fair wind, Herbert and his accomplice would be locked up by the weekend, meaning that David and Mally could go down to Tenbury Wells with uncluttered minds.

* * *

Bertha and Reuben had never earned much money, but they spent even less. When you were one of eleven children, as Bertha was, sleeping five or six to a bed like sardines, you grew up learning to be frugal. As a consequence of this, the pair had put aside rather a sizeable amount over the years, and had always dreamt of a caravan in the country, miles away from the industrial coal-mining town they lived in. They also wanted to give Ruby, Len and David a change of scenery, because money was tight, and holidays were expensive.

This was the perfect reciprocal arrangement, because they, unlike Len, could afford the caravan, and Len, unlike them, could drive. In due course, a caravan was purchased, much to everyone's excitement, and sited on a small field owned by the Inn next door, in the rural wilds of Tenbury Wells, Worcestershire. It was physically only thirty miles from Brierley Bank, but to David's family, Tenbury was not only set in another, more idyllic world than the one they knew, but also in another, more idyllic century. After work on Fridays, they could be there in an hour and living a different life, as long as the Austin Cambridge Shooting Brake didn't break down.

The caravan was a six berth, which was cosy, and it was lit with gas lamps. The site held around twenty other vans, and had a breeze-block toilet and shower building, but most importantly, the pub, always lively and full of local characters, was but a short walk away. The surrounding countryside was deeply rural and pungently agricultural; not like the neater, manicured countryside of Stratford or the Cotswolds Villages. In short, perfect heaven for a little boy. The only thing David could have added to this heaven on earth was company. He had doting parents who spoilt him as much as they could afford to, but this was no substitute for a companion nearer to his own age. He had always longed for a brother or sister, and had mentioned this often to his parents, but thus far, no business had resulted.

They were due to visit the caravan over the coming weekend to see that everything was in order before taking a break from visiting it over the miserable winter months, so David had asked his parents if Mally could go, to keep him

60

company. Feeling guilty, and finding the big-eared young lad pleasant enough company, they agreed.

Wednesday came, and after putting in its usual twenty-four hours of hard graft, went. Thursday, having got the gist by watching Wednesday closely, did exactly the same, but still no news had arrived from Scotland Yard. The two boys, who were in the woodwork room, hacking away at the local two-dimensional sheep population, were frankly puzzled by the tardiness of the boys in blue.

"They must have read it by now," said David, taking a rest from his sawing to swig at his bottle of lukewarm school milk. "The criminals could be halfway to Germany by now."

"Just a thought," frowned Mally. "Did we, in fact, remember to put our address on it?"

"Yes," said David. "Definitely. I don't get it."

"Well, it's Friday the thirteenth tomorrow," continued Mally. "Perhaps that's when they'll turn up in loads of Black Marias and get 'em. It won't be a very lucky day for Herbert will it?"

They laughed as they picked up their saws again, and laid into the sheep with a vengeance.

Friday, disappointingly, was every bit as free of coppers as the rest of the week had been, and the boys were beginning to think the worst. Maybe the address was wrong. Perhaps Sergeant Rhys had intercepted the mail somehow, and was out to silence them. Luckily, they'd be out of the way that weekend. Tonight was the night they went off to Tenbury, and both lads were looking forward to it.

Shortly after teatime, Mally duly presented himself at the door of the Day residence, backpack full of pyjamas, tooth brush, binoculars and his indispensable 'Observer Book of Birds'. (Pocket-sized edition, for easy identification in the field.) Both lads jabbered away excitedly at the prospect of seeing lapwings and pheasants by the truckload, not to mention slow-worms, badgers, moles and rabbits, all of which made a refreshing change from the usual diet of mangy starlings. Ruby and Len smiled benignly at the two boys as they packed their suitcase. They liked to see David happy. A quick visit to the shed to check up on the reclusive Darbishire concluded the domestic duties, and they trooped down to the garage to load baggage and selves into the car. A short while later, they rolled up at Bertha and Reuben's residence, shovelled them in, and away they went.

Travelling with Bertha was always entertaining, and Malcolm had been forewarned. Bertha didn't quite understand technology. She had never, for example, used a telephone, and would go to her final rest without once taking advantage of Alexander Graham Bell's most successful invention. Nor had she had ever owned a refrigerator. Her meat resided in a pantry under a sieve-like affair which kept the flies away, and she liked it that way. When it came to automobiles, Bertha had not the slightest inkling as to how they worked, but she liked to berate Len, who had driven since he was about six, on his various failings as navigator and pilot. When he drove through fairly tight gaps or on one-track rural lanes, she would insist that everyone within the car should move up a little in their seats, to help her son-in-law get past. When she wasn't offering useful tips to the driver, she was usually singing 'Ramona' at the top of her voice, or laughing helplessly at something or other that had 'started her off'. Reuben, meanwhile, would just allow himself a wry smile and look out of the window.

The trip to Tenbury was a pleasant one, but on a cold November night there was precious little to see, and it was dark for most of the journey. They arrived at the site around seven in the evening, parked next to the van, and Len opened up. He connected the gas bottle, lit the gas lamps, and the family, plus Mally, tottered in.

Inside, the gas mantles flickered with a cosy light, and the two boys shot excitedly into their room, which contained two bunk beds, a window and virtually nothing else. They quickly unpacked their belongings and threw them in a heap on the floor so that David could give his eager friend the guided tour. Mally was treated to the secret double bed that came out of the wall, the chemical toilet, (or 'Chemi-Khasi', as Len had christened it) the card table that magically became a single bed, the wardrobes, the wire coat hangers and the roof vents. It was obvious to the meanest intellect that David was over-excited. He'd never had a friend stay before, and it was a big deal. Malcolm, who was also beside himself at the prospect of being a real country boy for two days, made a decent job of feigning interest in his personal wire coat hanger.

After the necessary settling-in period, the family decided to pop over to the Olde Inn for a quick pint of mild, or in the case of the two youngsters, Vimto, accompanied by bags of crisps complete with the obligatory blue bag of salt (which was almost certainly sponsored by the makers of the mild).

Whilst India gave England the curry, and Italy the pizza, the Black Country gave it the pork scratching, but in nineteen-sixty-five no one except the citizens of that area seemed to want them. Those in the know, however, rated them highly, and scoffed at the rest of the world, who wouldn't have recognized a good thing if someone had put it in a bag and given it to them with a pint of beer. There was certainly a high percentage of Black Country folk settled on this particular site, and this could almost certainly be attributed to the fact that Ray, the pub landlord, stocked these delicacies, and also Banks's beer to help swill them down. This, to your average Brierley Banker, was as good a way of marking where the civilized world began and ended as any other.

The pub was in full swing when they arrived. Unlike the pubs in Brierley Bank and surrounding areas, there was no problem with children being in the same room as the adults. Children's rooms were often drab affairs, equipped with squeaky stools, sticky, pop-soaked tables, soggy beer mats and a dusty blackboard. This board was the only form of entertainment provided from early evening till eleven o'clock, when the children would be collected, covered in chalk dust, smoky-eyed and overtired, to walk home with their ever-so-slightly inebriated parents. Not so the Olde Inn. It allowed children into the bars, as long as they behaved of course, and the same applied to border collies, and even the odd sheep or goat. This was a different world, populated by exotic creatures, the like of which David and Mally had not seen before.

Typical of the clientele was Billy, the local farmer, who was slight of build, and high of voice. Male castratos in eighteenth century Italy would have killed for his naturally high voice, mainly because it would have allowed them to hang on to their prized possessions. Billy's voice was so high that often only his border collie could hear him. He would always appear mid-evening, with his shotgun and two dead rabbits over the shoulder, and put in an order for a pint of cider. This wasn't your civilized, refined Bulmer's or Woodpecker cider, but a locally made hell-brew, fortified with dead mouse shreddings, bits of fermenting apple and anything else the addled loony who brewed the stuff could find in the barn at the time. After a couple of pints of this concoction, Billy would negotiate the pitch-black narrow lanes in his tractor. Even more remarkably, he never appeared to pay for anything, preferring 'Ye Olde English System' of bartering. Dead rabbits and pheasants were slapped onto the counter, or the occasional box of apples, and the deal was done. Heaven knows how he paid for his tractor. Perhaps it was better not to ask.

One room in the pub was slightly more homely, with plusher chairs and less border collies per square foot, and this was where Bertha held court. A few stouts and she was on top of the big square cast-iron pub table, and very occasionally under it, singing 'Ramona', or possibly 'Are you lonesome tonight?' Unlike back at home, where licensing laws were keenly observed, here the customers partied well after last orders, safe in the knowledge that the local beat bobby was playing dominoes with his farmer friends in the snug and didn't possess a watch.

Around midnight, the happy band staggered back over the field, torches flailing wildly in all directions, to the caravan. Mally and David marvelled at the pipistrelle bats that dive-bombed them as they walked, missing their heads by inches. Bertha was so sloshed, she probably never noticed.

Tired children were made to empty their bladders into the chemical toilet, in spite of protestations that they didn't need to go, and then tucked into their bunks. The customary 'night-night's and 'God bless's concluded, they turned over and were asleep in seconds. Country air was indeed powerful stuff, just like country cider. The adults pulled beds from walls and revamped the furniture to construct their mattresses. A little unsteady on their feet, and giggling at their inability to remember how it all fitted together, they eventually settled down.

A lone fart, owner unknown, followed by Bertha and Ruby's inimitable laughter broke the silence, and then all was still and black.

* * *

After what seemed like ten minutes, Reuben was bringing the tea round.

At seven-thirty, the boys were dressed and exploring the area around the caravan. Bertha and Ruby were cooking bacon sandwiches while Reuben made yet more tea, and last but not least, Len was outside, fiddling with his dipstick. In short, all was right with the world, and that included the weather. None of them had expected much, it being November, but what greeted them was glorious sunshine, and a half decent temperature to boot.

After breakfast the boys were dispatched to the showers, clutching towels and soap. This was the quintessential caravanning ritual, and something that those who have experienced it remember for a lifetime. There is something about arriving at a draughty breeze-block construction with towel under the arm, and the prospect of an eccentric and unstable coin-metered hot water supply that stays in the subconscious forever. Memories flood back of troublesome moths the size of small birds, water that changes from scalding to freezing within seconds, sodden towels, and most depressing of all, the occasional stripe of excrement smeared up the toilet wall. Add to this, overly jolly men in white vests who whistle just a tad too cheerfully for seven-thirty a.m. and you have a vision of purgatory.

Two slightly tacky and hastily-dressed boys re-emerged some twenty minutes later and declared themselves reasonably clean and ready for action. Len suggested a trip into Tenbury with him in the car, whilst the others peeled sprouts and squirted Johnson's wax furniture polish everywhere. The lads could, Len suggested, do a spot of fishing on the Teme, and then look around the town. David asked if they could visit the toy shop at the end of the high street, because, due to one thing and another, he hadn't yet got hold of his Sopwith Camel. Mally said he was perfectly happy to do whatever.

Sandwiches were made, and David and Len's fishing equipment was hauled out from under the bunk beds. Mally's eyes lit up when he saw the split cane rods, creels, nets and assorted floats and ledgers. The fishy smells on the keep nets in particular, appeared to speak to the depths of his soul. They set off, and within ten minutes were in town and parked up by the river. The boys carried their equipment across the playing fields and excitedly set up their rods. Len advised them to use ledgers, rather than floats, and bait the hooks with balls of cheese.

By lunchtime, they had caught several large chub, and Mally had an almost evangelical look in his eye, as if he had discovered his Heaven on earth. They munched on cheese sandwiches, held with muddy, chub-flavoured hands, washed down with tea from Reuben's specially prepared tartan flask. Pigs in mud would have struggled to be happier. The fish, for those who quite rightly tend to worry about these things, were returned to the Teme, to be caught again the next day by someone else. It was their life and they seemed resigned to it. God had probably mentioned to them, when handing out his initial instructions to the flora and fauna, that they would be provided with a nice bit of cheddar on a daily basis, but the trade-off was to expect the odd sore lip. The fish, after carefully reading the contract, reluctantly agreed that it was the best deal they could expect and signed on the dotted line. A few, namely the edible ones, obviously didn't bother to read the small print.

Len, who fancied himself as a comedian and raconteur, told Mally about his recipe for cooking the famously inedible chub, which David had heard around seventeen times previously.

"You wrap it in silver foil along with onions, sliced potatoes and butter, placing it in a preheated oven for an hour. Then you get it out and throw it into the pedal bin."

Mally laughed like his holiday depended on it.

After a successful morning's fishing, they dismantled the rods, put them back in the car, and decided to have a look at the local cinema. 'Goldfinger', the latest James Bond film, was showing, and Len thought it would be good to come back that evening to see it, maybe followed by a pub dinner. He purchased four tickets because he knew that Bertha and Reuben would almost certainly prefer to go to the Olde Inn, and then they wandered down the high street towards the toy shop. Len excused himself for a few moments to look at a new pair of binoculars in the shop next door, so the boys walked into the shop, chatting about their potential purchases. They joined the queue behind an elderly lady in a pink bobble hat who was buying some postcards. She duly paid the shop assistant, and turned to face David.

There, large as life, and at least twice as ugly, stood Miss Kettle.

David's blood migrated south in a hurry, and didn't bother to leave a forwarding address. His face was a sort of greyish white, and his eyes were the eyes of a startled chub that had lost its cheese and found a hook. Miss Kettle looked at him for the briefest of moments and walked off down the street clutching her postcards.

"Dave," said Mally, concerned. "You look like you've seen a ghost. What's up?"

"I have. Didn't you see who that was?"

"No. I wasn't paying attention. I was looking at that wind-up Dalek in the window. Who was it?"

"That was the ghost of Miss Kettle."

Had this been a film, there would undoubtedly have been some dramatic music just at that point, but this wasn't a film. It was real life. The shop owner asked them what they wanted, but the boys never heard the words. They were in shock. Besides, toys could wait. This was serious. They backed out of the shop, breathing hard, and David had to sit on the window ledge to compose himself. This had thrown their plans into complete disarray. How could Scotland Yard arrest someone for murder when the victim wasn't dead? And *why* wasn't she dead? Nothing seemed to make any sense. It was at this juncture that Len arrived, and noticing his son's bloodless countenance, asked what on earth was up.

"Oh, nothing, I just felt a bit giddy!" replied David, and he wasn't lying.

"I'll get you both back," said Len, worried, "I told you not to eat your sandwiches after you'd been messing with those fish!"

The short trip back was largely uneventful, apart from a lot of conspiratorial whispering, which Len took as par for the course with eleven-year-olds. They rolled up next to the caravan, where a scene of perfect domesticity greeted them. Bertha, in her flower-patterned pinafore, was sitting outside next to an old green Formica-topped table with a pile of sprouts in a colander. Reuben was making tea for the workers, and Ruby was doing the crossword in Woman's Realm. It was probably where H.E. Bates got the idea for The Darling Buds of May.

"Ah! Len," she called, "Just in time. Five letters - to egg on."

"Is it 'toast'?" asked Reuben optimistically, as he stirred his teapot.

The boys had continued in conspiratorial mode, and were now prodding each other and saying, "You ask", and "No, you ask!"

"What?" asked Ruby, "If anything, are you two on about?"

"Yes," frowned Len. "What's going on with you two? You've been like secret agents all the way back. Talking of which, Rube, I've got some tickets for the new James Bond at the Royal in Tenbury. It's supposed to be the best ever."

"Mom," asked David eventually, his left foot stirring up the dirt of a fresh molehill, "guess who we just saw in Tenbury?" He'd remembered that his mother had walked down the road with him on the Saturday when Miss Kettle was missing from the shop, so this would be of interest to her. Ruby admitted that she hadn't a clue, but had a guess at Sean Connery.

"Stop being silly. We've just seen Miss Kettle, coming out of a toy shop!"

"Ah!" said Ruby. "You think you have. But you haven't."

David could make nothing of this, unless his mother had been at the local cider, and before the sun had gone over the yard-arm too.

"You saw Martha Kettle, not Edna Kettle," she explained. "Edna, who owns the toy shop in Brierley Bank, has got a younger sister; only a year or so younger, but she's the spit of her. Almost like twins. The only way you can tell is that Martha is a very pleasant woman and Edna's a bloody battle-axe - sorry for swearing, Malcolm."

"Well how do you know which one I saw?" asked David. "You weren't even there!"

"I'm certain," insisted Ruby, "because she lives here. That's her caravan, can you see? The old blue one right down in the orchard."

The boys could see the caravan.

"She used to own the wool shop in Brierley Bank years ago, but she lost her husband to cancer, and retired down here, like a lot of people from round our way have. Her married name was Onions, which she always hated, so she went back to being called Kettle when he passed away. From Onions to Kettle - out of the frying pan into the fire, if you ask me! I see her to talk to every now and then, and she's lovely. Mind you, Miss Kettle from the toy shop used to be okay at one time, according to Berth, didn't she, mother?"

"Yes, I went to school with her," said Bertha, wiping her hands down her pinafore. "They say she lost her fiancé in the war, and never looked for anybody else. She always wanted children, like her sister had, and she just got bitter and surly after that."

"Funny that she wanted to run a toy shop, and she hated kids!" observed Mally.

"Yes," agreed Ruby, "But we don't know how she was affected by what happened. I bet she's a nice enough woman underneath, if you take the trouble to get to know her."

"Bit late for that, unfortunately," said David, out of the corner of his mouth.

For the rest of the afternoon, the boys went off, exploring the country lanes and bridle paths, with mixed emotions running through their heads, caused by Ruby's explanation. They sat on a stile and tried to make sense of the latest developments. David, who loved to listen to Mr Lewis's tales from Shakespeare, likened his earlier shock in the Tenbury toy shop to that experienced by Macbeth at the dinner table, when the ghost of Banquo popped up to have a few words. Now that they knew the apparition was in fact Miss Kettle's sister, they felt better, if only for the fact that Plan A, the Scotland Yard letter, was still up and running. That said, they felt very guilty for feeling better, because, of course, it meant that Miss Kettle was now almost certainly still dead, and perhaps a nice lady after all, as Bertha had suggested; it was just that life had dealt her too many blows. This train of thought then led them to think about the Tenbury-based Miss Kettle, who seemed to be going about her duties totally unaware that her only sibling was no longer amongst those breathing.

"Wasn't that a weird coincidence?" asked Mally, sucking on a straw, country-style. "We saw her in another blooming toy shop."

"Yeah," agreed David, shuddering at the encounter, "I thought it was her ghost checking out the competition. And another thing! I've just realized that, with all that excitement going on, we never got to buy anything. I'm starting to think that God doesn't want me to have a Sopwith Camel."

They continued down the lane, pausing at a freshly dead pheasant. Mally prodded it with his stick. "Do you think your dad would let me take that home with me?" he asked, more in hope than expectation.

That evening they said their farewells to Bertha and Reuben, and drove off to town for the big film. The two boys sat spellbound, as Bond and Oddjob knocked seven shades of excrement out of each other, in glorious saturated Technicolor. They sniggered at the naked lady painted from top to toe in gold, and looked the other way when the kissing came on. The acting was pure cardboard, but they would be convinced, probably for the rest of their lives, that this was the best Bond film ever. Such is the power of childhood experiences.

It was precisely for this reason that the caravan had been bought in the first place. As loving parents, Len and Ruby tried to fill their offspring's world with as many happy memories as possible, because they realized these events would serve two important purposes throughout his life. They were certainly good while they were happening, but almost more importantly, they would become wonderful to recall, on the quiet, reflective days when there was nothing much else to do. They had learnt from their own experiences that a happy child helped to make a happy adult, and they worked selflessly, like two tired little sparrows feeding their ever-hungry chick, to make that happen.

Often, people only realize how truly happy they used to be when they allow themselves the time to dust off the distant memories and take another little peek at them. Sadly, happiness is always thought of as belonging to the past tense, and most folks seem to need a passage of time to elapse before they can accurately assess the true measure of their happiness. Maybe rose-tinted spectacles should be offered on the National Health, so they could all be happy in the present, without having to wait.

* * *

Len drove back to the site with Ruby sitting next to him in the front and the boys chatting excitedly in the back seat. Having abstained from alcohol for far too long, the driver suggested that they pop in for a quick one at the Olde Inn before turning in for the night. As they parked up and locked the car, Ruby could hear Bertha in the pub's lounge some twenty yards away, blasting out a spirited rendition of Ramona. If she was to get anywhere as a singer, observed Len, it was perhaps a good idea to expand her repertoire.

Ray was doing a roaring trade, it being Saturday night, when all the local farmers and farm hands were letting their hair down, if one could describe a game of three card brag and a pint of Banks's Mild as letting one's hair down. Rabbits were flying across the counter in exchange for beer, scratchings were consumed in vast quantities, and a good time was being had by all. Mally, in particular, was having the time of his life, because this was precisely the world he wanted to live in. Just as David instinctively felt different to the factory workers, and knew he would one day be an artist, so Mally knew he was in the wrong place back at

74

home. He was a country boy through and through, and it was going to be a hell of a job wedging him back into that Austin Cambridge come Sunday teatime.

The remainder of the evening, though hugely enjoyable, was virtually a repeat performance of the previous evening. If brevity is indeed the soul of wit, as Mr Lewis believed, then what happened next could be summed up with the words, ditto midnight, ditto bats, ditto bed, ditto flatulence. And then Saturday closed its eyes, and fell into a deep sleep.

Some things can be relied upon. Day turns to night, night turns to day, and Reuben will make cups of tea somewhere between the two. David was even beginning to warm to the idea of tea at six-thirty. Sleeping, he reasoned, was no fun if he was fast asleep, because he was not in a position to appreciate it. The experience was far more rewarding if someone had broken into that sleep and allowed him to have another crack at it soon after.

Mally, who was not a fan of tea, had expressly asked to be left out of this ritual, preferring to get his beauty sleep. With ears like that, reasoned Len, he probably needed his full eight hours. David reckoned that the pipistrelles had singled out his friend the previous evening because they thought he was a large, enemy bat. Kids can be so cruel sometimes.

Sunday began with a hearty cooked breakfast, after which the boys disappeared into the countryside. After crossing several stiles, they came across a ford, which neither of them had ever seen before. It crossed a small lane in the hollow of a pair of hills, and was shallow enough to wade through. They found an old rusty bin, full to the brim with spent shotgun cartridges, and it was as if they had discovered buried treasure. They stuffed their pockets with them, so that they could make gun belts like the cowboys wore, when they got home. David liked to fit them into his right hand whilst pretending to hold a rifle, and catapult them over his shoulder, as if ejecting them after firing. He was good at making *ricochet* noises, as were most boys, and he sneeringly pointed out that the girls at school just couldn't do them properly. Mally concurred, but conceded that boys couldn't skip, knit or play hopscotch, so that was fair. He had bought some Bazooka Joe bubble gum while he was in town, and he was blowing huge bubbles, some ten inches across, as he ploughed through the tall grass, imaginary gun in hand. David, who had sneakily broken a hawthorn from a bush, surprised him by popping the bubble, so that Mally ended up with a sticky pink plastic-like layer over his entire face and fringe. Oh how they laughed, when Mally had eventually forgiven him.

Across the field, in the distance, was a derelict house, which was obviously a farm building of some sort. They ran across to it with a view to exploring the old place. What must have once been a cottage garden was now full of old farm machinery, rusting away and patently unused. There is nothing that speaks to the soul of a young boy like a deserted house, especially one in the middle of nowhere. They tried the peeling old front door, and finding it open, crept inside. The wallpaper was faded and dropping off the walls and the floor was made of large, uneven quarry tiles. There were musty, drab Victorian pictures still on the wall, a small table with a vase, and some long-dead flowers. David and Mally tiptoed through the hallway, into a large, farmhouse kitchen. It was full of cobwebs and clutter, with chipped pots and pans all over the place. Stray cats had obviously taken over, and two of them were sidling up to David's leg, demanding attention.

"It's like that story about the ship," remarked Mally. "The Marie Celeste."

David admitted that he was not familiar with it.

"Well, it was an abandoned ship, floating about in the fog, in the middle of the sea at night, and when these sailors got on board, it was creepy, like the crew had left in a hurry. The food was still there, and the drinks, but no people."

David, who had developed an aversion to both darkness and fog, began clutching his groin in earnest, desperately in need of a lavatory. Suddenly, they heard a strange, screeching, high-pitched ghostly wail, which sent cold shudders down their spines. They stood rooted to the quarry tiles with fear.

"What are you doin' in moi bloody house?"

Billy, shotgun in one arm and the obligatory two dead rabbits in the other, was silhouetted in the kitchen doorway, casting an ominous long shadow and blocking their exit. David opened his mouth, but his voice had unexpectedly taken a short break, and had not left a note to say when it would return. He looked like one of the fish they had caught earlier, struggling to breathe in the keep net. Mally offered to help, but all he managed was "Mwar!" which did not significantly add to the debate.

"Ain't you Bertha's young 'un?" asked Billy, softening by half a percent.

"Er, yes," spluttered David, who's voice, thankfully, had returned early, due to unforeseen circumstances. "We -we thought it was a derelict house!"

"Well thank you very much, you cheeky young buggers. This is how we lives round here. I bet you lives in a bloody castle, don't you?"

"Council houses," chipped in Mally. Economical maybe, but better than his previous "Mwar!" by a long chalk.

"Well, you ain't nicked nothin', and I knows yer granny, so bugger off before I loads me shotgun!"

The boys didn't need to be told twice. They shot out of the house and over the field, David clipping half a second off his previous best, which one will recall was the 'five hundred yards up a steep hill in fog' handicap. Mally drew up behind, due to his carrying a few extra pounds and having had his first half-a-cigarette the previous Thursday. They paused at the stile, panting furiously, hearts pounding like African drums in their chests.

"Bloomin' heck!" gasped Mally. "Is life always this exciting with you?"

David panted a half smile and wiped the sweat from his brow.

"And another thing," continued his flushed accomplice, his huge ears red hot. "If that's what farmer's houses look like, I've changed my mind about being one!"

It was two marginally more composed youngsters that sauntered into the caravan an hour later, just as Bertha's Sunday dinner was being served up. They quickly washed their hands and sat down to eat, telling the assembled group all about their exploits, but excluding the house-breaking incident. They hoped, next time they were at the pub, that Billy would do likewise.

The boys spent the afternoon quietly, bird watching and playing football. After a final cup of tea and a piece of Bertha's home-made bread pudding, the bedding was packed away, the gas bottle disconnected, and the caravan mothballed until the spring. Mally, in particular, was very sad to be leaving, but Len told him that he had been very well behaved, and was welcome any time. One by one they squeezed into the old car, and with its suspension down to the floor, it groaned its way across the site with a defiant puff of blue smoke, and was gone.

CHAPTER 8

One Lump or Two?

Mr Lewis greeted the class, marked the register and began his English lesson. He had long admired the Bard of Avon, so today was a special treat for him. He was about to introduce his little dears to the many joys of one William Shakespeare. At eleven years of age, he couldn't afford to destroy their interest forever by reciting vast slabs of soliloquy at them, much as he would have liked to, so he decided to ease them into it with a few interesting facts.

"So, children, who can tell me what Shakespeare is famous for?"

A sea of erect arms, like a scene from a Hitler youth rally, greeted him, along with multiple "Sir sir sirring".

"Helen."

"Sir, sir, he wrote films, sir."

"Not quite, Helen. Films weren't invented in Shakespeare's day!"

"Sir, sir, how come I saw one then?"

"Well, Helen, the plays he wrote were so popular all over the world, they later made them into films," replied Mr Lewis patiently.

"Well sir, I saw it, and it didn't mean anything. The words were all funny," said Helen, looking a bit 'told you so-ish'.

"Ah!" said Mr Lewis, warming to his subject. "That's because these plays were written hundreds of years ago, and they are written in the English that was spoken at the time. If you go back even further, to Robin Hood's time, the language is even more difficult to understand."

"Then how come I can understand Robin Hood on the television, sir?" asked Helen, sensing that outright victory was in her grasp.

Terry Deakin, silent up until now, suddenly began singing, "Wobin Hood, Wobin Hood, widing froo the gwen!"

Mr Lewis bit his lip and persevered. He explained that television's Robin Hood was not quite as authentic as it might have been, and moved on.

"Who can tell me where Shakespeare lived?"

The Hitler youth began saluting frantically again.

"Sir, sir, Stratford sir!"

"Very good, Sandra. Mr Perriman and I were thinking of arranging a school trip to Stratford to visit Shakespeare's house. You can see all sorts of interesting things there, including his will. Do any of you know what that is?"

"Sir, sir. It's what he leaves to his family when he snuffs it."

"Excellent, Simon, though I don't much care for your choice of phrase. Yes, his will, which you can read for yourselves, left a sum of money, around fifty pounds, to one of his friends, which was a lot in those days. He left some money for the poor people of Stratford, and he left his second best bed to his wife! The interesting thing though, is there are only six Shakespeare signatures in the world, and three are on his will."

"Wow sir!" said Mally. "That's really rare! That's rarer than a dodo's egg."

"Yes it is, Malcolm. Well done. Yes it is."

At playtime, David and Mally sat on the radiator by the woodwork room, drinking their freezing cold school milk.

"Why is this stuff never right?" moaned Mally. "It's either got lumps of ice in it, or it's turning into cheese. Yuk!"

"No news from Scotland Yard yet," said David dejectedly. "I bet they won't come."

"And I bet they will," replied Mally confidently. "Perhaps they're busy, what with Myra Hindley and everything."

They finished their milk and returned to the woodwork room to work on the last sheep. The Nativity play was looming. Each day, in the main hall, children were practising their lines and positions. A dedicated band of parents were running up various costumes for shepherds, wise men and general bit-part actors, and Mrs Hancox was putting the recorder ensemble through their paces. All that now remained for her to do was just get them to sound musical.

The choir were also coming along very nicely, and the readers were almost word perfect with their lines. David had promised Mr Perriman that his sheep would be on schedule, if not on budget, and the scenery painters, headed by Mr

Weston, were in full flow. Everything was ship-shape, as Mr Perriman liked things, but one would be forgiven for thinking that the weight of the world was on his shoulders, had one seen him slip into his office, put his head in his hands and sigh, as he was now doing. He scanned a piece of paper disconsolately and stared out of the window.

* * *

David got home at around four o'clock, demanding cheese sandwiches and soup, as usual. His love of cheese was such that he would have gladly come back in the next life as a chub, had it not been for the bit about the hooks. After tea he went into the shed to socialize with Darbishire, his new hamster. Two minutes later, he was back in the house, squealing with pain, with blood gushing from his finger.

"The little monkey's bitten me!" he cried, his usually excellent knowledge of anthropology failing him momentarily. "I put my hand in to stroke him, and he attacked me. He's not friendly like the other one was. He's vicious!"

Ruby washed the finger and put a plaster on it.

"He just needs to get used to you, David," she said. "He needs more handling."

"Well you can flipping well handle him next!" sobbed her son, who wasn't the bravest when it came to physical pain.

This unpleasant incident reminded her to pop out the back door to call her neighbour and thank her for feeding the hamster while they were away. It was Frank who appeared, as his wife was busy eating her dinner.

"No problem, Rube," he said, "Nasty little thing though, compared to his last one. It bloomin' bit me, and fetched blood!"

Ruby offered her sincere apologies, and assured him that if it bit anyone else she'd flatten the little thing with a rolling pin. After tea, Ruby asked David to run a little errand. She'd promised to drop some potatoes up to Bertha's house, and had forgotten. As an incentive, she promised him a bit of extra pocket money for his trouble. David didn't mind, because he wanted to go past Miss Kettle's place and see what was going on. It had been empty for a week or more now, and he felt sure people would be taking notice. He grabbed his bag of potatoes and made his way up the high street. As he approached the shop, he could see that the lights were on, which was curious. Maybe someone had taken the shop over, or the police were in there, investigating the crime scene.

He tried the front door, which was open, and walked in. There was no one in the shop, and if he had been familiar with the expression *déjà vu*, he would probably have been using it at that point. He stepped nervously through the gap in the counter, and called into the back room.

"Is anyone there?"

There was no reply, so he took a peek behind the counter, and froze to the spot. The till was open and empty. Lying prostrate on the ground, with two big bumps on her head, was Miss Kettle.

CHAPTER 9

Till Death Do Us Part

David stared incredulously at the limp body. What is often referred to as the gamut of emotions from A to Z ran through his mind, as he tried to rationalize what he was experiencing. There were more questions than answers. If Miss Kettle was dead, and carted off by Brierley Bank's own Burke and Hare in a plywood coffin, why was she back in her favourite position? Surely, if she'd been lying there unnoticed for a week or more, she'd be a skeleton by now. He wished he'd drawn a chalk line round her the first time, like the police did, to see if she'd moved.

If the large plywood box didn't contain the cadaverous Miss Kettle, what *did* it contain? And why had she grown another lump? She had two huge bumps on her head now, one fresh, the other fading a little, and they had done nothing at all to improve her looks. He worried for a split second that bumps were contagious; she was certainly amassing a sizeable collection. It was then that he noticed that she was breathing, the shock of which nearly caused him to do the opposite. Her black cardigan was definitely heaving up and down. The Boy Scout and the Coward within him had a brief moral argument, which the Scout won by a whisker.

David knelt down beside her and tried to lift her up, but she was a dead weight, and far too heavy for him. Thinking quickly, he reached for a small, stiff piece of card which he had spotted under the counter, and began to fan her with it. The thought of administering the kiss of life was too frightful to bear, but luckily her eyes flickered, and she came round. He pocketed the card and gulped audibly.

"You bloody little bugger!" she slurred.

David had expected a tad more gratitude for his efforts.

"You bugger," she repeated, groggily. "You hit me over the head with a cricket bat!"

"I didn't!" he cried, indignantly. "I'm helping you up!"

The strength was returning to her body, and she began to scramble up off the floor.

"Bloody bugger!" she repeated. "Bloody little bugger!"

David didn't hang around to discuss their grievances. He grabbed his potatoes and ran as fast as his weedy little legs could carry him. He was last seen hotfooting it in the general direction of his grandparents' house, shaving yet another fraction of a second off his latest record, which you will recall, was set just after leaving Billy's house in Tenbury. Miss Kettle rose unsteadily to her feet, clutching her aching head. She hadn't a clue why she had been laying spark-out on the floor, or what had given her the huge, angry lump right at the top of her brow. Her thoughts were far from clear, but she was of the definite opinion that that little boy had attacked her with what she believed to be a cricket bat. He had then run off, but before doing so, raided her till.

The good news was that she recognized him, and knew where his parents lived. What a stroke of luck that she'd come round in time to see him. Something he obviously hadn't bargained for. She'd had her suspicions before about this character ever since he'd walked into the shop one day wearing a balaclava, and bought a cap gun. Perhaps he had been planning to raid the Post Office, but was also casing her joint at the same time. She could only speculate. Well, he had met his match this time, she swore. The police would be informed, as would his parents, and it was only a matter of time before he was eating bread and water in an Antipodean penal colony.

Miss Kettle was not having a great time, what with one thing and another. Only a week or so previously, she had been wrapping up business at the end of the day, and was in the process of emptying her big brass till, ready to transfer her takings to the bank. She had put the cash into a large cloth bag, taken it into her private rooms at the back of the shop, and then returned to pick up a half-crown which she had dropped on the floor. The old lady's hands were a little shaky and she was always dropping things, which was annoying. After bending down to retrieve the aforementioned coin of the realm, and, forgetting that the till was still open, she shot skywards like a rocketing pheasant, only to connect with sickening force with the underside of it. The impact was so powerful that she went out like a light, and fell to earth she knew not where. She resurfaced around seven in the evening, unsure if she was still Miss Kettle or Napoleon. The blow to the head had addled her thinking and was causing her to have dizzy spells and sickness, so she thought it wise to consult the doctor, whose premises were a few doors away.

Doctor Olga Rodgerson, who closely resembled James Robertson-Justice in a tweed skirt and had the abrupt manner to match, took one look at her and condemned her as unfit for consumption. She ordered her to take a week off and close up the shop, and when Doctor Rodgerson said jump, you meekly asked 'How high?' Miss Kettle staggered back to her shop like a Brierley Bank chain-maker on a Friday night at closing time, and grabbed a piece of card and a pen. Barely able to remember her name, let alone compose a notice, she scrawled a few words on the card, and tossed it in the general direction of the counter, while she went in search of Selotape. She came back from the private room at the back, armed not with the Selotape but a pink bobble hat, and then proceeded to study it from every angle, in the vain hope that it would reveal to her the reason it had been picked up. She then closed that line of enquiry, and decided to lock up and turn off the light instead. Groping her way around the perimeter of the room in pitch darkness, she negotiated the stairs on all fours and somehow managed to find her bed.

The next morning, bright and early, she had somehow managed to pack a small bag of clothing, and, still feeling very queer, zigzagged off down the high street in search of Cradley Heath Railway Station. There was a nine-thirty train to Kidderminster, where she could get a connection to Tenbury Wells. She hadn't seen her sister for a while, and this was the perfect excuse to catch up and recuperate in the country. A week later, on Sunday the fifteenth of November, feeling much more like her old, grumpy self, she returned to the shop, ready to do battle with the filthy unwashed public on Monday morning.

CHAPTER 10

A Right Herbert

Herbert Rhys was fretting about his lost dog. This simple statement, without further clarification, would give the impression that he was a caring and considerate individual, and he wasn't. What he was really concerned about was the lost revenue from his lost dog, or more correctly, bitch.

The Staffordshire bull terrier was, and still is, the dog of choice for all right thinking Black Country men. Not for them the effeminate little Cavalier King Charles, or the cosy Labrador. No, they needed a dog that had muscles, a beer-belly and tattoos, just like them; a dog that could fight another man's dog. A dog that's all man, even if it's a woman.

Physically, Herbert's terrier conformed to all these criteria. She was muscle-bound, strong, and decidedly ugly like her owner. She was also, to use the popular northern expression, as daft as a brush. She was gentle, and wouldn't dream of harming a fly, even if it was doing something unspeakable on her dinner. As such, she was a dreadful disappointment to her owner, who reminded her of this with the odd kick, when it pleased him. Herbert was always keen to make a few quid, illegal or otherwise, as long as it didn't involve mental effort - for which he was patently ill-equipped - or hard work. His friend, a Brummie barrow-boy spiv named Sammy Chinn, knew a friend of a friend who had a male bull terrier, predictably named Satan, and he had heard that Staffs puppies sold for decent sums.

Seeing their opportunity to make a buck without doing very much, this odious twosome had arranged for the two dogs to be introduced at a house in Old Hill. It was to this end that Ugly, for that was her given name, was being manhandled into Sammy Chinn's old van on the foggiest night Brierley Bank had seen for years, and she was not liking it. Maybe Ugly had her heart set on a quiet night in front of the T.V., or perhaps she wanted to stay in and wash her hair. One can but hazard a guess, but one thing was certain, and that was, she didn't care for Sammy Chinn and his robust dog-handling techniques. Having made it abundantly clear that she had no intention of getting into a strange man's van, (she was not that kind of dog) the sheepskin-coated lowlife became overly persistent. Usually, with people like that, a quick growl from Ugly did the trick, but this character would not be said. He was getting too rough, and fists were being employed. Every dog, mild or otherwise, has its breaking point, and Ugly had reached hers. She tore about ten quid's worth of value from Chinn's coat, and left his leg looking as if he'd been exfoliating with barbed wire. At this point, he thought it advisable to loosen his grip on this Hound of the Baskervilles, which then promptly made for the wide-open spaces.

Rhys and Chinn, looking even more like Victorian body snatchers than usual, searched high and low in the nearby fog-bound graveyard, calling the dog's name, but it was well gone. They walked down the high street towards the toy shop, discussing, with great annoyance, the potential loss of income from the sale of the puppies.

"Never mind," said Chinny, once the pair had calmed down. "Put a notice in the shop windows, and somebody'll find the bloody thing. We'll have to tell my mate that the date's off, and we'll rearrange it as soon as we can. At least we can make a few bob on tomorrow's house clearance."

The following day, they were due to clear some furniture from a lady's house in the high street, next door to Miss Kettle's shop. Chinny, who was a lorry driver by trade, had a sideline, clearing houses. He liked to think of himself as an antiques dealer, but really he was a low-grade rag and bone merchant. He would clear out the houses of the deceased and offer some derisory amount for the job lot, to a grieving relative who didn't realize the true value of the items being disposed of. Chinny would brag that the punters insisted on keeping worthless junk for themselves, but sold him priceless antiques for peanuts. Anyone so ignorant, he argued, deserved to be ripped off. The lady whose house he was clearing that Saturday, for example, had let him have the huge grandfather clock for a few measly quid, but insisted on keeping her old photos and letters, which were worthless. He'd knocked together a protective box for the clock, and already had a rich buyer who was willing to pay him a hundred pounds, no questions asked.

After all their 'missing dog' enquiries had drawn blanks, Herbert eventually decided to follow Chinny's advice, and put notices in shop windows. It was to this end that he walked into Miss Kettle's place on Monday the sixteenth of November, and rang the bell for service. Miss Kettle, charming as always, came out from the back room, and asked him why he'd rung the bloody bell.

Herbert told her about his lost dog, and reached into his pocket for one of the cards, but realized that he'd used the last one in the butcher's shop. Miss Kettle begrudgingly found him an old piece of card from the floor below the counter, and Herbert began the painful task of writing out his notice. He was not one of life's high flyers, and writing was not one of his strong points. Miss Kettle drummed her stubby fingers on the counter impatiently, and told him to keep his bloody revolting tongue in his head, as he was salivating on her work surface. The job done, he handed her the card, and reluctantly parted with a shilling, her weekly fee for such notices. She grasped for the coin, and, as usual, let it slip through her sausage-like digits onto the floor. Bending down to retrieve it, she surfaced at a rate of knots and connected with the opened till doing around twenty miles per hour. Had Miss Kettle been conscious, and she was far from it, she might well have been saying to herself, "Silly me, I've been and gone and done it again!" or words to that effect.

Herbert Rhys, never slow to realize a good thing when he saw one, though slow in just about every other respect, reached over to pocket the contents of the till, and was gone, seconds before a certain young boy ventured into the shop once more, eager to spend his pocket money.

CHAPTER 11

The Long Arm of the Law

Chief Inspector George Boyden sat behind his impressive, polished wood desk, sipping tea from a very nice china cup. He reached for a biscuit, just as a polite knock came at his door. A pretty lady police sergeant entered, carrying mail.

"Ah, morning, Susan," said George, spraying crumbs across his desk, and smiling apologetically at his messy biscuit-eating technique.

"Morning sir," she replied. "Your post. These are private, for your eyes only. This pile I've taken a look at; nothing earth-shattering, I'm afraid – and you didn't win on the Premium Bonds again, so you're still a Chief Inspector, and stuck with us lot!"

"Ah, well!" he sighed, taking another bite out of his chocolate digestive. "I'll cope. Anything else, Sue?"

"Well, there is one thing, "she said, smiling. "We received this today. My first instinct was to bin it, but I don't know. Maybe….."

"Let's take a look," he said, and she handed him a dog-eared cream envelope with a lapwing printed on the flap. He took it and looked at her questioningly.

93

"It's a strange one, Guv. Probably just a silly child playing about. It's been round the Wrekin. Seen the address?"

He smiled, and took out the letter, reading it twice, while Sergeant Sue stood silently. Finally he looked up. "Well, I never!" he said. "Well I never!"

Chief Inspector Boyden had the kind of flattened accent of a man that had been to University and lived away from his place of birth for a long time. It was largely nondescript, but if one had an ear for linguistics, traces of a Midlands accent could be detected. Occasionally, he would let a clue slip. Once every five years or so, he'd say 'sheed' instead of shed, (or spill) as in, 'Did you sheed my tea?' and hastily correct himself when officers looked blankly at him. Now and then, he'd hear himself say 'her' when it should have been 'she', much to his embarrassment.

If the ghost of Sherlock Holmes had examined George Boyden's office, looking for vital clues, he would no doubt have concluded;

"My dear Watson, the man we seek was born within five miles of Dudley, but he has spent his adult life in London. He makes a mess when he's eating biscuits, he is a leader of men, well-liked and respected. He has dark hair, receding on top, and he probably doesn't have a wooden leg!"

And, if one excuses his indecisiveness about the leg, he'd have been spot on.

"It's *very* funny, Sue," said the Chief Inspector, "but I can see why you want me to take a look. We should never take anything for granted, right? Better to be safe than sorry, for the sake of a quick phone call to Staffordshire. I agree with your instinct, but the reason I said 'well well', was because I happen to know the people mentioned in this letter. This is most awkward."

He invited her to take the weight off her size-nines.

"This Sergeant Rhys was an old pal of mine, when I was down in the Dudley area, years ago. He's a dead straight copper, and could have done okay at a higher level, but he genuinely preferred being a beat bobby. He runs a small town single-handedly, and sorts out the troublemakers the old fashioned way. They respect him for it too."

Susan looked puzzled. "What about the accusation, sir? It's childish, I know, but sort of serious as well."

"Sue, if Charlie has had anything to do with whatever this lad is suggesting, I will eat my uniform, and run round Scotland Yard naked shouting 'Up the Albion!'"

Susan giggled. "Why 'Up the Albion', if I may ask, sir?"

"Well," he laughed, "I'm a Wolves fan, and we hate the buggers!"

People discard accents when they relocate, but seldom their club.

"Look Sue, seriously now," he continued, "leave this with me. I'll make a quick, diplomatic phone call, just to see what on earth's going on. I trust Charlie. I don't know his son, so I can't comment, but if I know Charlie - and I do - if his son's been up to anything, woe-betide him when Charlie finds out."

CHAPTER 12

An Inspector Calls

David Day, having offloaded his King Edwards and swigged a cup of Camp Coffee at his grandparents' house, just to steady his frayed nerves, shot off down the hill like a whippet, homeward-bound. As he neared the toy shop, he thought it wise to cross the road and stream past as quickly as possible, closely scrutinizing his Eagle comic as he ran, to disguise his features. He had no cause to worry, as Miss Kettle was upstairs, applying vinegar and brown paper to her brow in the hope of reducing the swelling. Shortly afterwards, she hobbled up the hill to the tiny police station, to seek an audience with Sergeant Rhys.

Tuesday morning woke at its usual time, and declared itself ready for business. House sparrows tweeted contentedly, the sun came up, and David was getting outside of a few rounds of toast, prior to beginning his short walk up the road and through the alley to school. He was totally confused now about the Miss Kettle incidents. He kept trying to focus on the possible scenarios, but his brain, like Brierley Bank, was foggy. He instructed it to concentrate, but all he was doing was repeating the word 'concentrate', and not really concentrating at all.

Point 1. He was quite pleased that Miss Kettle appeared to be alive.

Point 2. How did she become alive again, after she was dead?

Point 3. If the two men weren't carrying her in a box, what did the box contain?

Point 4. What would happen if Scotland Yard came looking for a dead woman who was alive, and two murderers who hadn't killed anybody?

Point 5. How long would he and Mally have to do in jail for wasting police time?

He shuddered at the prospect, and sought Mally out in the playground to ask his advice. Once Mally was abreast of the facts, his admirable solution was for David to go home at the end of school and tell his mom and dad the whole convoluted tale. After all, he and Mally had only been acting in everyone's best interests, and it was a hard parent who could chastise them for that. David reluctantly agreed. The plot was indeed thickened considerably by the previous night's goings on, but the best policy was to come clean. In the back of his mind, he hoped and prayed that Miss Kettle had had time to think things over, and had dropped the cricket bat theory. It was plain that he was going to have to avoid the old dragon for a few weeks, and then purchase his Sopwith Camel wearing a false beard. The only snag with that idea was that the only place he could get a false beard from was Miss Kettle's shop.

At four o'clock the final bell was tolled. All over the school, chairs were placed on desks, satchels were loaded up, and children of all shapes and sizes stampeded for the exits, ignoring the teachers who were yelling at them to walk, not run.

David said goodnight to Mr Lewis - for he was a polite and considerate young man - and enquired as to the health of the new dog. Mr Lewis replied that she was lovely, and admitted that he had not yet actively sought the real owner, as he had been busy. This brief exchange concluded the teacher-pupil dialogue for the evening, and they bade each other a fond farewell.

This was David's favourite time of the week, because Tuesday was comic day. Every week, on the button, his choice of reading matter would appear through the letterbox, but it would be evening time before he had chance to read them. He was a Dandy and Beano man, naturally, but he also liked the Beezer and the Eagle. He was lying on the living room carpet, legs intertwined and feet in the air, totally engrossed in a juicy Dan Dare episode, when the front door knocker rat-a-tat-tatted with military precision. Whoever was without had a disciplined mind, and did not suffer fools gladly, if at all. Ruby took off her pinafore and strode purposefully over to answer it. David followed, heart in mouth.

"I wonder who that can be at this time of night," she asked, to no one in particular.

"There's only one way to find out," replied Len, practical-minded as ever.

She opened the door a few inches, and saw Sergeant Rhys.

"That's the bugger!" shouted Miss Kettle, pushing past both of them and storming into the room, her walking stick waving furiously. David, by this time, had done the quickest about-turn in history, and was aiming for the back of Len's cosy armchair, and relative safety.

Following her into the house came Sergeant Rhys and Herbert Rhys, in the order named.

"Miss Kettle, Miss Kettle," the officer called. "Leave this to me, if you please!"

Miss Kettle halted her advance. "He's the bugger!" she reiterated, pointing her walking stick as if aiming a gun at David's trembling head. Len got up out of his chair, and raised himself to his full six feet. He was clad only in a vest and trousers, having shed the dirty working clothes, and looked to the myopic casual observer as though he could handle himself. As Miss Kettle was only four-foot-eleven in her curlers, she presumably thought it unwise to proceed.

"What on earth is going on?" asked Len. He was a quiet man, but he didn't like this mass invasion after a hard day's sawing and filing.

"I'm sorry for that outburst, Mr Day," said the sergeant. "Miss Kettle is a little annoyed, and with good cause. Not long ago, I received a phone call from an old friend of mine, a Chief Inspector Boyden of Scotland Yard. He has been sent a rather peculiar letter."

"Oh Gawd!" groaned David from behind the armchair. He put his hands over his head, and emitted a pitiful whine.

"This letter was written by your son, David. In a nutshell, it accuses my son, Herbert here - say hello Herbert."

"Hello," said Herbert, dully.

"As I say, it accuses Herbert of murdering Miss Kettle and stealing money from her till."

Ruby and Len just stood there with their mouths wide open. They turned to stare at David, with incredulous looks on their faces. He had his head in his hands, trying to avoid all eye contact.

"As you can plainly see, Mr and Mrs Day, Miss Kettle is not, by any stretch of the imagination, dead. In fact, if she will forgive me, she is looking decidedly animated. Would you not agree?"

Ruby and Len nodded dumbly, in unison.

"Furthermore, this letter has embarrassed me and my family, and cast aspersions on our good name. It didn't just cast a few local aspersions mind you, oh no! It just cast them all the way to the Chief Inspector at Scotland Yard. That's all!"

Len looked at David, with what is best referred to as an exasperated expression.

"Son, firstly, is this true? No, forget that. It's true. How could anyone make it up? You have done some interesting things in your time. Most of the time you are on a planet all of your own, and I don't mind. There's nothing wrong with a bit of daydreaming. It's good for you, I firmly believe that, wouldn't you say, Rube? But this?" he paused, as if he had suddenly lost his ability to construct sentences. There was a great commotion within his voice box area, as if ten thousand words were struggling for pole position on a grid that only comfortably held twenty. Outwardly it came out as a kind of strangled gargle.

"But WHY?" he eventually croaked. "What on *earth* did you write it for?"

All this time, Miss Kettle was just staring at David, which was extremely unnerving.

"W-W-Well," he stammered, his matchstick-thin body shaking visibly.

"And what is more," continued Sergeant Rhys, "Miss Kettle assures me that she has never seen Herbert before in her life."

Herbert, who had been looking decidedly sheepish all along, suddenly looked extremely relieved, as if a heavy weight had been unexpectedly lifted from his tiny mind.

"A person she *has* seen, however, is young David over there. She saw him as she was coming to, after he had clobbered her with a cricket bat."

"That's definitely him," glared Miss Kettle. "That's the little bugger what did it!"

Ruby had, until now, been taking this quietly. David was quite capable of sending a crazy letter to Scotland Yard, for some bizarre reason best known only to himself; she could accept that. However, hitting an old lady over the head with a cricket bat - that was where she drew the line.

"How *dare* you accuse my son of that, you bloody stupid sod!" she stormed, the sleeping giant now awake. "How *dare* you take the word of this stupid battleaxe against his?"

Sergeant Rhys recoiled dramatically, like a salted slug. He appeared to have shrunk from six-feet tall to around four-foot-eight. Miss Kettle looked at him, hoping for a gallant response. None came.

Suddenly, without warning, David spoke.

"Did you say that you'd never seen this man before, Miss Kettle?" he asked, with just a whiff of Perry Mason about his delivery.

The room went quiet.

"Never clapped eyes on him. I'd have remembered a fizzog like his."

Herbert, for some reason, hated being the centre of attention. He began to look out of the window.

"Then what do you suppose this is?" David continued, retrieving a small piece of white card from his blazer pocket. While all the commotion was going on, the cogs in his head had been grinding and whirring. He remembered some of the wording on the card, and it struck him as interesting. He proffered it to Sergeant Rhys.

The card read:

NOT WEL.

BUMPON HED. CONCUSED.

GON CARVAN.

BACKIN WEEK.

Sergeant Rhys studied it carefully. He could glean nothing from it. His facial expression was clearly saying 'So what?'

"Turn it over," suggested David helpfully.

The other side read;

BLACK STAFF BULL TERROR MISING.

ANSERS TO UGLY.

CONTACT H. RHYS.

CAIRE OF POLICE STATON.

"What does that tell you, sir?" asked David, the very model of the polite but ruthless detective. If he had possessed a little waxed moustache, he would have twirled it.

"Well, it tells me the one who wrote it was an awful speller for a start," said Sergeant Rhys, looking over at his son with thinly disguised contempt. "Apart from that, not much."

"You see, sir, your son Herbert said he had never been in Miss Kettle's shop in his life, and she said she didn't recognize him either. Well, he *did* go in, because he gave her this card to advertise his missing dog. If you notice, sir, he's written it on the back of Miss Kettle's old note about when she hurt herself, so he's telling a fib, sir."

Herbert was looking increasingly uncomfortable, as if he needed the toilet in a hurry.

"Well why on earth didn't Miss Kettle recognize him? Answer me that?" asked the Sergeant, perplexed.

"I don't know, sir. Maybe when she came round, she lost her memory."

Ruby and Len, who both looked as if they had been reading a complex novel and discovered they'd inadvertently skipped a chapter, were desperately trying to keep abreast.

"*Did* you lose your memory, Miss Kettle?" asked the Sergeant.

"How the bloody hell do I know, you stupid bugger?" she snapped, "I wouldn't be able to remember."

"I think it's best you tell us your version of events, son," said the copper. "We're just going round in big circles here!"

David explained how he'd gone to the shop on the first occasion, to buy his aeroplane model, and found her lying on the floor. He thought she was dead, and ran back into the fog, where he heard Herbert and Chinny talking. He now admitted that he'd probably put two and two together and made sixty-seven.

"They were talking about hitting the ugly 'b', and how she was biting them and scratching," said David.

Miss Kettle looked as if she was about to take exception to being described as an ugly 'b' but she bit her lip.

"Then, the next day I saw Herbert and his friend with Miss Kettle in a coffin, loading her into a van, but now I realize it wasn't her, obviously, unless she was born again, like Jesus."

A pedant would probably have asked how all three of them could squeeze into one coffin, but the tale was complex enough, without diversions. Herbert, silent throughout, finally gave tongue, and several dollops of saliva in the process.

"It'th a mithunderthanding," he spluttered. "I wath talking about my dog, Ugly. Thee bit and thcratched Chinny, tho he hit her."

The front rows hastily donned waterproof clothing, in anticipation of his next sentence.

"The big boxth was jutht a grandfather clock. We'd juth done a houth clearanth!"

This seemed to placate his angry father to some extent, but he still seemed perplexed.

"That's all well and good. I understand all that, more or less, but why was Miss Kettle unconscious?" he asked, his already florid complexion turning a shade more violet. Miss Kettle nodded in agreement. Why indeed? She needed answers.

"Well" said David, desperately trying to pick up the threads again. "I think I understand what happened. This note says that she wasn't well, because she'd bumped her head, so she'd closed up and gone to the caravan. When I was in Tenbury, I thought I saw her in the toy shop down there, with a pink bobble hat on."

Miss Kettle appeared to be coming out of her mental fog.

"That's *right!*" she said. "I bumped my head on the till. I'm always doing it, but it was a nasty 'un that time. I went to my sister's to rest."

"So it *was* you in the Tenbury toy shop," said David triumphantly. "Mom said you were your sister!"

The sergeant was by now plum coloured.

"Anyway," continued the boy, warming to his theme, "The second time, I went in again, to see who was looking after the shop now that Miss Kettle was dead, and I found Miss Kettle on the floor again, with *two* bumps on her head. The old one, I suppose, and a new one; fresh, it was. I noticed her breathing, so I tried to wake her up, and I fanned her with this bit of card which I found on the floor. I reckon she wrote it out and forgot to stick it in the window and Herbert wrote on the back of it, so that proves he *did* go into the shop."

"But why was she unconscious again?" asked Ruby," I'm totally confused."

"I don't know," said David. "Perhaps she whacked her head again. She just admitted that she's always doing it. I didn't hit her with a cricket bat, dad. I haven't got one, for a start. I left mine at Ludlow Castle. Maybe Herbert did, and because she was a bit groggy she thought it was me."

The silent one spoke up.

"I bloody well didn't, thee brained herthelf on the till again."

Herbert realized, as soon as the words left his mouth, that this amounted to a confession. Sergeant Rhys looked at his boy through narrowed eyes, like a hungry cat eying up a flea-ridden starling on a bird table.

"I can't say I remember your Herbert, 'cause I don't," said Miss Kettle. "I remember the young lad though, 'cause I've seen him about, in my shop and in Tenbury. Perhaps he's telling the truth. He *was* fanning me when I came to, I admit. If he'd hit me with a cricket bat, I daresay he wouldn't be fanning me, come to think of it."

The old lady was in full flow now.

"I can't recall who was there, as I say, but what I do know is that my till was full, because I'd had a busy day, and when I came to, it was empty, so which one of these nicked my cash? Answer me that!"

Sergeant Rhys turned to Herbert, and asked if he could have a brief private word, out of earshot of the assembled party. He apologized, and the two withdrew through the back door to the small rear garden. Those present, eager not to miss anything, dashed over to the rear window, the extremely diminutive Miss Kettle jostling for a ringside seat. Meanwhile, in the garden, Sergeant Rhys appeared to be pointing out a particularly interesting blue tit which had settled on Gladys's fence post, next door. Whilst Herbert turned to see it for himself, the dextrous officer extracted his truncheon from its holster, and, in no time at all, planted it forcefully on the back of his idiot son's skull.

The results were spectacular and instant. Herbert's legs appeared to fold up like a decorator's trestle table, and his carcass hit the turf with a dull thud. For the time being he was sleeping nicely, and taking no further part in the immediate proceedings. The good officer sheathed his trusty weapon and came once more inside.

"I will have that cup of tea now, Mrs Day, if you don't mind," he said, and removing his helmet, sat down for the first time. He was acting as if very little had happened.

"Right, young David, I owe you an apology, and I think you owe me one too."

David knew what was coming.

"Next time you need help, you must confide in your good parents here right away, and you must also come straight to me. If you thought that I'd protect that useless waste of God's oxygen outside, you've done me a disservice, young lad! Still, you were only doing what you thought was right, eh?" He turned to Ruby and Len. "He's a good lad, your David. He might be a bit of a daydreamer, but his heart's in the right place. Now, Miss Kettle, I think you've got something to say too."

Miss Kettle stared at the carpet. "Er, yes. I've been a bit of an old fool. Sorry young 'un."

"That's okay, Miss Kettle," David beamed. "Sorry about your head!"

"And a big favour folks," added the honest copper, replacing his headwear. "I have no right to ask, but can we keep all this to ourselves? I didn't quite follow official procedure just now. If you tell me how much was missing from your till, Miss Kettle, I'll give you double, and then that's the end of it, okay?"

Miss Kettle arrived at a figure that took into account personal injury and inflation, and shook on it.

"And now folks, I'll just finish my tea and then collect the remains. I'll see myself out. Come on, Miss Kettle. I'll give you a lift up the road."

He returned to the garden, and hauled the stupefied Herbert up from the ground. The officer virtually carried him through the outhouse and threw him into the back of his police car. The Day family waited in silence until the car drew away. Finally, Len spoke.

"Well," he said, blowing a little. "Never a dull moment with our David, eh?"

CHAPTER 13

The Antiques Roadshow

Len, resplendent in brown cow-gown, was attaching his micrometer to a chunk of metal, and 'tut tutting' to himself. His latest machine tool was giving him some design problems, but he was a quietly determined man, and he knew he would crack it eventually. David's father had worked at the firm for virtually all of his life, after a stint in the army, doing his national service. His own father, now dead, was a jovial, deeply sarcastic Tommy Trinder look-alike who smoked far too many Woodbines a day, and succumbed to a massive and deadly heart attack as a reward for his efforts. His mother, who was prone to depression, had never enjoyed a single day of her life, and made her husband's life a misery. Ironically, she was still going strong, and Len, ever the doting son, fetched and carried for her and was never thanked. He had been a bright lad at school, but the family were poor, and he was never encouraged to seek a good education. He had passed for Grammar school, but his best friend hadn't. The friend had begged Len to come to the secondary school, so that they would not be parted, and Len, being Len, agreed.

Thus, his destiny as factory fodder was guaranteed, which was just as well, as his parents couldn't afford the uniform and books anyway, and he was told in no uncertain terms that work, and the money it earned, not fancy schooling, was what he needed. His own upbringing had made him determined that David would have the best education he and Ruby could afford, and he would be encouraged in whatever he wanted to do. This was radical and enlightened thinking for Brierley Bank in nineteen-sixty-five.

If David wanted to be an artist, that was okay by them. They also realized how important it was to feed a child's imagination. That was why Len spent his hard-earned cash on all the bits and pieces of bric-a-brac. They taught him about ages gone by, which was a good thing. In truth, Ruby and Len spoilt him rotten, but insisted that his manners were impeccable. That's why Ruby *knew* he hadn't whacked Miss Kettle with a cricket bat. He just wasn't the type.

The tool-room door swung open, breaking Len's concentration, and in swaggered Sammy Chinn in his sheepskin coat and Aston Villa scarf. Two sovereign rings the size of cast-iron pub tables adorned his dirty fingers.

"Watcher, Lenny!" he beamed, smacking him heartily on the back, and sending the sensitive micrometer crashing to the floor.

"Steady on Sammy," moaned Len, "They cost a lot of money."

"Never mind that," he said, "I got summat for yer!"

Sammy, a lorry driver, was officially delivering steel to Len's firm, but he also sold bits and pieces of furniture and curios purloined from his house clearances to anyone who was interested. Len acquired most of the stuff he took home for David from Sammy. He would have not been pleased had he realized that old ladies and the naïve were paid a pittance for them, for Sammy to sell on at a handsome profit.

"Sign here, Lenny boy!" said Sammy, offering him a delivery note for the latest batch of metal. "Now howsabout this for your lad?"

He fetched in a rough oak box of around one and a half feet square by six inches deep. The rusty hinges, which were crudely made, looked ancient and primitive. The box too was very old and smelt musty.

"I did a house clearance in Henley in Arden - very posh area, Lenny boy. Some old girl was clearing a cottage in the high street; it was her sister's place. She was ninety-five when she snuffed it, and the sister - who looked even bloody older - she'd come from miles away to supervise the clearance. There was clocks, paintings, books, rugs and allsorts. The antique firm got the best stuff, but they let me clear the loft out, and I got the stuff they didn't care for. I've done alright out of it though. Could have done better if the old bugger hadn't involved the bloody antiques firm, mind you!"

He opened the musty box.

"I thought your lad might like these. You said he loves calligraphy and writing and that. These are just old deeds and letters. They must be well old though. You can't make head or tail of the writing. You know; 'I owest thou the sum of ten shillings, forsooth,' and all that malarkey. I thought he'd like them to copy the writing, 'cause you told me he was becoming a master forger!"

Len smiled. David had recently purchased a thirteen-colour biro, and he loved to copy pound notes with it. He was convinced that the forgeries were so good that they could be

111

passed in shops, and his indulgent parents pretended to agree, just to please him. They had also got him a calligraphy set for his birthday, but as yet, he had not had chance to experiment with it, possibly because his life had been a big social whirl just lately, what with one thing and another. Len asked how much, and Sammy fleeced him for a couple of quid and was on his way, once he'd persuaded Len's young apprentice, Eric, that a Victorian badly-stuffed weasel in a cracked glass box was a wise investment.

That evening, Len took his latest treasure home, and David excitedly unwrapped his calligraphy set. He laid out the various old documents on the floor, and decided to try and forge one of them. His dad had insisted that, just for a change, he refrained from 'improving' the items by adding flourishes and illustrations to them. He had seen too many of David's 'improvements'; the blue saxophone being still a vivid and painful memory.

Father and son prepared some paper to make it look as old as the originals. Len took some of David's cartridge paper from his sketchpad and tore the edges against a steel rule to give them a hand-made look. Then, he asked David to get him some cold tea from the pot. The paper was soaked in this brew to give it an aged look, and left to dry by the fire. Len also sprinkled instant coffee granules on the wet surface so that they would look like the 'foxing' marks on very old documents.

The results were impressive. David loved when his dad spent time with him, showing him things, as often, after a hard day's work, he was too tired to do so. To the untrained eye, the blank page now looked four hundred years old. Father and son were so pleased with their handiwork; they made several more, improving their technique with each subsequent page. Len advised David to dip his nib pen into brown ink, and dab his writing periodically with a blotter, which gave the impression that words had faded, and added another touch of realism. Best of all was when his dad, who was now quite enthused by it all, showed him how to add wax seals by dripping sealing wax onto the paper and pressing small coins into it before it solidified, just like the Sheriff of Nottingham did on T.V.

For the rest of that evening, David beavered away at his desk with his tongue sticking out at a jaunty angle, forging his documents. Ruby turned to a bit of knitting, whilst Len settled into the armchair, and sleep engulfed his tired frame.

CHAPTER 14

Bill the Quill

The first lesson of the day, after registration, was double English, which David always enjoyed. Mr Lewis had given them a project on Elizabethan England after introducing them to William Shakespeare the week before. He told them all about the many well-known phrases and sayings that had survived from the era, and he was keen that the children should visit Stratford, maybe after Christmas, when things were a little less hectic and the Nativity play was out of the way. He wanted to visit not only Shakespeare's birthplace, but also Anne Hathaway's cottage and especially Mary Arden's house, which he rated as being the better of the three properties.

Mr Lewis's sheer enthusiasm for the subject was infectious, and he sensed the children were quite eager to get cracking, which was gratifying. This feeling was borne out when David stayed behind during playtime to show his teacher something he'd done the night before. Mr Lewis was desperate for a coffee and a biscuit, but such was the lad's excitement, he gladly went without.

David took a folder from his satchel and proudly opened it, to reveal what looked remarkably like an old document, complete with red seal bearing the octagonal threepenny bit design with portcullis motif, to add that extra touch of class.

"What is this then, David?" asked Mr Lewis, smiling broadly. "An Elizabethan letter?"

He'd already discerned that it was a David Day forgery, but he was mightily impressed with the technique, nonetheless. He kept silent, so as not to steal the lad's thunder.

"It is, sir!" said David, chest swelling with pride at the ease with which he had fooled his teacher. "But there's just one thing, sir. I drew it last night, sir!"

"My Goodness! It's brilliant, David," exclaimed Mr Lewis. "How on earth did you make the paper look so old?"

David proudly explained his methods, as if he'd been familiar with them for years. Mr Lewis asked if he could read it, and David readily agreed, but warned his teacher that it might prove to be a difficult task. He explained that he had copied it from a real old document, and he could not make head or tail of it. The spellings were all wrong and the sentences were strange, and some of the letters were hard to decipher too. Mr Lewis said that this was because the language had changed over the years, as had the handwriting styles, and often, documents such as wills and deeds were particularly complex anyway.

He put his reading glasses on, and instantly realized that David's handiwork was not an old, stuffy legal letter as he had imagined, but a poem. He had a go at the first verse.

Life's wearing patternes, etched upon your face,
Hath never forced my loving gaze away,

While fickle lovers fear the march of yeares,

So I will love thee stronger with each day.

Mr Lewis turned to David and removed his glasses, a large smile spreading across his face.

"Thoughtful of you to choose my favourite author, David, being as we're studying him this week. Which play was it from? Remind me."

David said that he didn't know, and looked a little puzzled.

"Did you get it from that book in the library that shows the Shakespeare manuscripts as he wrote them, with all the crossings out and mistakes and everything? It's a fascinating book isn't it? I don't recognize the quote. Is it from the Sonnets or poems section?"

David wondered which wavelength Mr Lewis had moved to. He certainly wasn't sharing David's anymore.

"No sir, you don't understand. I copied it from a real old document. My dad got it for me. It's not from a library book. It's a real letter. I've got loads more too, in a really old box. Shall I bring them in to show the class?"

Mr Lewis said that would be a *very* good idea, and, there being no time like the present, he asked if David could pop home at lunchtime and get them. David agreed - it was no problem, as he lived at the back of the school, and it would take five minutes.

"Oh, by the way, sir," he added as he turned to the door, hoping to snatch the last few minutes of playtime. "I think I know who owns your dog. In fact, I'm sure of it."

Mr Lewis's face dropped. This wasn't what he wanted to hear.

"Sir, this is a bit secret. This man is not very nice. I'd better not say who he is, but I know that he doesn't treat the dog very well. It's been kicked and punched, sir, and that's why it ran away."

"Are you sure about this, David? It's a serious accusation you're making, my lad!"

"Sir, I'm certain. Ask my mom and dad if you like. They know about it; Sergeant Rhys knows about it too. Honest sir! I know you like the dog, and she'd be much better with you."

"Thank you very much, David. I might just hang on to her and do nothing till I'm contacted, in that case, eh son?"

David and Mr Lewis smiled knowingly at each other and they went their separate ways, one in search of a game of football, the other in search of coffee and biscuits. Mr Lewis hit the staff room with around three minutes to spare. He went over to the sink, swilled out his cup with the dragon motif and threw in a spoonful of instant coffee and some hot water and lime scale from the old kettle. He was just prising open the biscuit barrel when he was aware of Mr Perriman at his side.

"Hello Mr Lewis," he said. "I wonder, have you got five minutes at lunchtime? There's something I need to talk to you about. Just between us for now. It's a bit concerning, to be truthful."

He smiled a sad smile, and lumbered off back to his study.

Mr Lewis's brow knotted with thought. Mr Perriman was usually a cheerful old soul, so something was afoot. Like all

117

conscientious people, he wondered if he'd done anything wrong himself. Was he about to be sacked? Surely not! Had word got round that he had wilfully stolen a dog? Was old man Perriman about to retire and appoint him as the new Head? He slurped his disgusting coffee and ruminated as to what this could mean.

After playtime, David went to the woodwork room to put the finishing touches to his small flock of two-dimensional sheep. At last, after many weeks and five times as many jigsaw blades, they were finally completed, so he recruited Mally to help him carry them into the hall ready for the dress rehearsals. As they paused to open the hall door, a round, peach-cheeked little creature answering to the name of Brian Tubbs waddled past.

"What you doin'?" enquired the rotund one.

"We're knitting a hot water bottle out of spaghetti; what do you think we're doing?" explained David. He had inherited this devastating use of sarcasm from his deceased paternal grandfather.

"No you're not!" said Tubby, stating the blindingly obvious, "you're carrying three wooden sheep into the hall. I'm not stupid! Listen, I've got a joke. Adam and Eve and Pinchmee went down to the sea to bathe. Adam and Eve was drowned, who do you fink was saved?"

Mally and David looked heavenwards in unison, Mally adding a 'Tch!' to better indicate the sense of boredom with something they'd heard a million times.

"Sorry Tubby, can you repeat that? Adam and Eve and who did you say?" asked David, smiling angelically.

"Pinchmee!" said Tubby.

The two shepherds immediately set upon the child, pinching him all over his chubby little body, until he was forced to flee, and threaten, from a safe distance of course, that he was going to tell his dad, who, by all accounts was twice as large, and twice as good at fighting as their dads were. Bucked up by this brief bit of sport, the boys continued to herd their flock into the hall, finishing the task just as the dinner bell rang. David made his excuses and dashed home to collect the documents for Mr Lewis to see, and hopefully show the class. They might, he hoped, possibly even gain him points for Yellow House, and make up for the ones he'd lost by turning up late after the mini-hurricane incident.

He burst into the house shouting "Mom, Mom! It's only me," and realized he'd interrupted his mother having a quiet cup of tea with his Aunt Deirdre. Deirdre was Bertha's sister, but she was as unlike Bertha as it was possible to be without changing sex and growing a big beard. Ruby asked him to say hello to his Aunt, which always quietly annoyed him, as he was fully intending to do so of his own volition anyway.

Deirdre had come for the club book.

Ruby was an agent for Rattanwood's Catalogue, a weighty publication that enabled customers to purchase all manner of goods by parting with a small sum each week, usually over a twenty-four week period, thus easing the financial burden. David liked the front covers of these books, which were usually reproductions of famous works of art. The current cover girl was a rather fetching young thing wearing a pearl earring, by someone called Johannes Vermeer. In the past, the book had featured Constable's Haywain, which David had copied faithfully with his coloured pencils. He also liked to look at the men and women within, with their cheesy expressions and cardboard leather jackets. Usually, these Ansell's Bitter Men types would be engaged in matey chat, and pointing to something interesting that was happening out of camera shot, and if they weren't doing that, they were complimenting each other on their flared corduroys with the big belt, or their choice of chunky wool jumper with leather football motif buttons. Slightly more disturbing were the pages where these same gentlemen were still continuing their discussions, but now clad only in Y Fronts. Far better, thought David, were the pages dedicated to ladies' underwear, which he would often study in depth when his mother was outside, helping Len to clean the car.

Deirdre had come to borrow this encyclopaedic volume in the hope of procuring some slacks for her husband, Bill, who came from a generation that allowed their wives to dictate their apparel. For whatever reason, and David suspected shame, this emaciated and overly-fussy creature lowered her voice to an almost inaudible whisper when she mentioned 'The Book'. She could be talking with relative gusto about her son Graham's New Estate Car, or Bill's Hernia Operation, but as soon as she turned her conversation to borrowing The Book, the volume was turned down to a whisper. In stark contrast, her son, the aforementioned Graham, spoke incredibly loudly, especially when using the telephone, which often prompted Len to comment that if he spoke just a little louder, he wouldn't actually need the help of the damned instrument.

Deirdre was looking concerned about the cost of the weekly repayments, and was whispering to Ruby about the possibility of extending them from twenty-four to thirty-six weeks. Ruby patiently explained that the trousers probably wouldn't even last that long, and suggested that she might rent Bill's trousers instead. The barbed comment flew about a yard above Deirdre's head, and she continued to dither and browse over her cup of tea. David made his excuses, collected his oak box from the kitchen table and headed back to school. Meanwhile, Mr Lewis had kept his appointment at the Head's study. He tapped the door, and hearing the words, "Come in," duly did so.

Mr Perriman was sitting at his desk, head in hands. He looked up to greet his friend and colleague, and silently proffered an official-looking letter for him to study. Mr Lewis read it twice, his face becoming ever more grave as he read.

"What do you think we should do, Dai?" said Mr Perriman, after he had given him time to digest the contents.

"Never say die, for starters," replied My Lewis stoically.

"Sorry, I mean Mr Lewis," said Mr Perriman, puzzled at his old friend's sudden insistence on formality.

"No, no, I meant, never give up, Sam. It sounds awful, but can't the council cover the costs?" he asked.

"Afraid not, Mr Lewis - er, Dai. That part of the school is built on old mine workings. This whole area is riddled with them. They've condemned the old science block as of now, which means the kids will have to walk up to Thornwood School for science for the time being. The rest is unaffected, but the entire roof is shot and we've got hundreds of window frames going rotten all over the place too. The council have a modern, brand-new school up at Thornwood with tons of room for all of us if they build their new annexe as planned. No Dai, we're finished here, I'm afraid."

"But Sam, this is a really lovely old place with lots of character. It's small, it's homely, and the kids and parents

121

just adore it. We can't let this happen. I don't bloody well want to amalgamate with Thornwood – no offence to them, of course, but it'll become a huge, impersonal place, for God's sake!"

Mr Lewis was beginning to realize the full meaning of the letter, and his anger was rising.

"I don't either, old son," agreed Mr Perriman, close to tears. "I've decided to retire, Dai. You'll probably be made Head, if that's what you want. Thornwood only has an acting Head at the moment, and if we amalgamate, I'll recommend you highly, you know that. I'm about ready for the quiet life now. This is the last straw for me."

Mr Lewis felt very sorry for him, and didn't quite know the right words to say. It had obviously been a terrible blow to the Head, and had Miss Kettle been present she would no doubt have sympathized, having experienced a similar problem herself on more than one occasion. Mr Lewis explained that he had to get back to his lesson, and left the sad old man to his thoughts.

Meanwhile, David had breezed back into the school with his old oak box. He met a dejected Mr Lewis on his way back to the classroom for afternoon register.

"What's up, sir?" asked the thoughtful little boy. "You look fed up."

"Oh, nothing David, nothing," he lied. "Let's have a look at this here box then. That should cheer me up a bit."

The children were beginning to return in ones and twos from the playground, flushed from their football, hopscotch and skipping games. Mr Lewis and David stood together at the teacher's desk and opened the box. It was lined with a once-white sheet of paper, which had become water-stained

122

and yellowed with age. The paper that was glued to the inside of the lid was cockled and lumpy, and coming away in places. Inside the box there were documents written on thick parchment which were largely legal in nature, with old wax seals at the bottom, some dating back to the early sixteen-hundreds. Underneath these were several letters and documents written on paper, which were much more fragile. Some were falling apart on the folds, while others further down had fared a little better.

"This looks fantastic!" said the teacher. "How did you get hold of all these?"

David explained about his dad, and the house clearance.

"Which one did you copy?" asked Mr Lewis. He was virtually salivating with anticipation. This was his era. To him, this was treasure trove.

David found the page and carefully handed it to his teacher. Mr Lewis studied it closely, reading and re-reading the words and muttering to himself. David found another page and handed it over.

"Oh dear me, I need to sit down!" the teacher suddenly gasped. "Oh, bloody hell! Sorry David, I meant blooming heck!"

The children, who had sat down and were waiting for the register to be called, looked on in amazement. They had never heard a teacher swear. Some began to titter with their hands over their mouths.

"Sorry children, it just slipped out. Look, Helen, take the register will you? You know how it's done. I need to go somewhere with David; I'll only be five minutes. The rest of you, get on with your reading book, 'Lives of the

Elizabethans.' And no talking, or Cinderella will be visiting bottom-land, is that clear?"

The children confirmed that it was.

Mr Lewis flew down the corridor and into the staff room with David pacing behind, struggling to keep up. They sat down in a corner and the teacher took a deep, fortifying breath. He looked shaken, and for that matter, stirred.

"David," he eventually said, holding both the boy's shoulders and staring at him intensely as he spoke. "This is *really really* important. I don't want to raise your hopes, but I think - and it's only my untrained eye remember - I think what you have here is some of the greatest treasure that this country has ever seen. I think these documents were written by William Shakespeare himself!"

David stared back in disbelief. Mr Lewis's eyes were now looking a little crazed and darting all over the room. Beads of sweat began to form on his brow, and his hands were visibly shaking as he picked up one of the papers.

"This paper here is a letter from a friend, to a man named Will. The date is exactly right. This one is a sonnet - that's like a poem, David. The style is just spot-on for Shakespeare. These others are parts of writings. Who knows? Parts of plays! This one - oh my goodness! Oh dear me! This one is signed William Shakespere. He's missed the 'a' out, but don't let this concern you; he often spelt his name in different ways. Oh my life! These are worth a fortune, if they are real. That's the key, David, *if* they're real!"

David just gawped. As Mr Lewis waxed more and more lyrical, so he became less and less capable of speech.

"Why is the lining of the lid so lumpy?" asked the teacher, now at something approaching fever pitch. "There's something under this lining, or I'm a Dutchman."

David was surprised that his teacher's choices were so limited, but didn't mention it. That said, there are worse things in life than having to be a Dutchman. Vincent van Gogh was one for a start, and so was Johannes Vermeer, apparently, the man they'd asked to illustrate the Club Book's front cover.

Mr Lewis carefully felt the contours of the bulge that was hiding behind the lining paper.

"Whatever it is, son, it's very flat. Maybe it's another hidden piece of paper."

Being careful not to destroy the box's lining, he slipped his fingers inside a corner that was loosened, and connected with what felt like a hard, bony stick. He pinched it with his thumb and forefinger, and pulled as forcefully as he dared, and out it came in one piece. It was a bedraggled, but utterly wonderful old quill pen. Mr Lewis now knew what Howard Carter must have felt like all those years ago, when he opened up the tomb of Tutenkhamun. He carefully re-examined the loose lining paper, and seconds later, he removed a small slip of very old paper. It read;

'Thy final task is o'er now, and thou can'st take thy rest,

Now thou hast penned Will's will, old friend,

Sleep sound within thy chest.'

"David," said his teacher, in a voice now hushed and reverent. "This old quill pen is the very one that he wrote his will with, and probably many of his works. Do you realize what this is worth, if it's real?"

David, being only eleven, and not *au fait* with the cost of things, hazarded a guess in the region of a hundred pounds. His teacher laughed, and then suddenly his face became very serious indeed.

"This, my boy, if it is not some awful hoax, is priceless."

"What, not even a hundred pence then?" asked David, disappointed after the momentous build up Mr Lewis had given it.

"No no no!" the teacher spluttered. "Priceless! It means, well… very pricey!"

David was none the wiser. Mr Lewis was having a breakdown. He was sure of it.

"Look, David," he continued, rising shakily from the staff room chair. "You'd better run along and join your class. I'll be back in five minutes. Would you mind if I put these in the safe, just for now? I want to make a phone call, and then I'll be with you. There's a good lad. You're a prefect, so try and keep 'em quiet for a few secs."

David ran back to join his friends, and Mr Lewis picked up the phone in the staff room.

"Oh, hello," he said, his voice thick with emotion. "Could you get me the number for the British Museum please?"

CHAPTER 15

Darbishire Goes Walkabout

David got home at four o'clock, starving, as always. Mr Lewis had asked if he could hang onto the box, and bring it around that evening in the car. David, trusting his teacher implicitly, agreed. He also agreed to keep quiet about their little discussion and not even tell his parents, for fear of giving them false hopes. The teacher promised that he would explain it to them properly that evening, when he returned the goods.

While his mother prepared the tea, David popped into the shed to see Darbishire. He liked his new hamster, of course, but it was a lot more temperamental than Jennings. One minute, he'd be taking a seed out of the hand, the next he would be biting the hand that was trying to feed it. Highly strung just about summed him up. Len had recommended taking him out more and handling him, to get him used to people. This was all fine and dandy, but a hamster's bottom tooth is a solitary, hypodermic affair, and when they bite someone, they stay bitten. Experienced vetinarians who are used to dealing with ferocious feral cats and snarling, rabid Rottweilers, lose sleep worrying about the prospect of examining a temperamental hamster.

Blissfully unaware of this, David took a gamble and carried the creature out onto the front lawn, where he could show it off to a few assorted urchins that were playing ball games in his small *cul-de-sac*. Darbishire, unusually, was being very well behaved.

The urchins, having spotted a big boy with a hamster, were drawn to it like iron filings to a magnet, and before long there was a neat semi-circle of snotty-nosed, raggy-arsed and grimy-looking children all eager to stroke it.

"Can I hold him?" asked Urchin One.

"No, just stroke his back gently," replied David, the responsible pet owner.

"Can I give it a seed?" asked Urchin Two.

"Yes", agreed David. "He'll probably keep taking them off you, because he stores them in his cheeks till he's hungry. It's really funny, because his face keeps getting fatter!"

Urchins One, Two and Three were all supplied with seeds, which one by one were posted into Darbishire's eager mouth. Such was the interest in the animal that the Urchins and David didn't even bother to watch the old green and red steamroller that was trundling along the main road that adjoined the *cul-de-sac*. These relics of a bygone age were still occasionally flattening tarmac in order to earn their weekly pay packet, and usually when one of them put in an appearance, people came out to wave it on. The steamrollers were always crewed by a couple of characters that looked like Casey Jones and his boiler man, with flat caps and dirty faces, and they would always toot the steam whistle on request, if any passers-by particularly wished to hear it. This they now did, just as David had decided to break his own rule, and transfer the unruly and reluctant rodent to the clutches of the persistent Urchin Number One, just for a quick hold. The noise of the steam whistle seemed to deeply unnerve the twitchy little hamster, which appeared to place the blame squarely on Urchin Number One, and duly applied the full force of his hypodermic lower tooth to the boy's filthy little hand as punishment. The effect was dramatic. The Urchin squealed so loudly that folks in nearby Dudley would have heard him, and blood was gushing out of him in an impressive way. The hamster, which until that point was being held tenderly and with love, was now discarded like a red-hot jacket potato.

"Little bastard!" screamed the foulmouthed boy, who was, by now, in danger of becoming seriously anaemic, as blood gushed from him like crude oil from a Texan oil well.

Darbishire hit the deck heavily, and after a second or so to get its bearings, scurried off as fast as his half-inch legs would allow him. What happened next had a sickening inevitability about it. David could only look on in horror as Darbishire ran straight in front of the steamroller. He called out "Darbishire, watch out!" as if that would do any good. A second later, it was all over. Casey Jones and his boiler man waved cheerfully at the kids, and wondered why they just stared dumbly, and didn't reciprocate. Could it be, they mused with some sadness, that the public's fascination with steam was finally over? David dashed over to the back of the roller, just in time to see his pet being processed at the other end. It was flatter than a cartoon flat animal. Len would have needed his micrometer to measure him accurately.

David, wiping distraught tears from his face, pushed his way through the silent urchins and into his house. There was no point in arranging a burial this time, and definitely no point in putting Darbishire in a sock by the fire. He couldn't even claim the remains - they were stuck to the road. He broken-heartedly gave his parents the bad news, and they took it in turns to give him a hug.

"I think you'd do better with something a bit bigger," suggested Ruby, running her hands through his hair, as he gradually downgraded his grief from cascading tears to that occasional shuddering sob that is guaranteed to break the meanest heart. Len looked on sadly, and then went to fetch his shovel from the shed. An hour or so later, David was feeling a little better, but the horror of the creature's demise kept haunting him. His only comfort was that it was very quick and very final. Darbishire, the stroppy hamster, didn't know what had hit him.

David ate about half of his tea and sat quietly drawing in his sketchpad, the shuddering sobs having reduced their frequency to one every fifteen minutes, like the aftershocks of a particularly violent earthquake. The doorknocker sounded, and he rushed to answer it, because he knew that it was Mr Lewis.

The hour produced the man, and it also produced his new dog, Lady. She came bounding in, without as much as a 'by your leave' and jumped up to kiss David full on the mouth, a sensation that he was in two minds about.

"Get down, Lady!" shouted Mr Lewis. "Sorry David. I haven't had a chance to teach her any manners yet."

Teacher, dog and old oak box entered.

"Hello folks!" said Mr Lewis brightly. "I can leave her tied up outside if you prefer. She's friendly but boisterous!"

The Days said that she was welcome, and ushered them into the small living room. A visit from the teacher was on par with a visit from the doctor or the Pope. Len and Ruby looked pleased and nervous in equal measure.

"Sit down, Mr Lewis," said Ruby. "You'll have to excuse the state of our house; we've just had our tea."

Mr Lewis dismissed her concerns with a kindly wave of the hand.

"Give it to us straight," said Len. "What's he done this time?" David shot his father a scornful look.

"No, no, David's fine. He's one of my best pupils as a matter of fact. I wish they were all like him, I can tell you," smiled the teacher, pausing to accept a cup of tea and a biscuit. "No, I've come to see you about this here oak box. I told David, as a favour to me, not to mention it till I arrived."

Ruby gave David her 'Here we go again with your not confiding in us' look.

"You don't look too happy, David, if you don't mind me saying so," observed Mr Lewis, noticing the odd stray tremor from the previous sobbing session. "You look a bit flat, son."

"Not half as flat as his hamster," thought Len to himself, as he sat down in his armchair to hear the latest news. Very unlike Len to miss a joke opportunity, but this wasn't the time, he felt.

"He's just lost his pet hamster," explained Ruby.

"Oh, I'm sorry, David," said his teacher. "Anyway, on to brighter things eh? Folks, I don't want to build your hopes up. I'm no expert, and it could all be an elaborate scam, but I can't see for the life of me how it would benefit anyone if it were. No, that wouldn't make a scrap of sense."

"Neither do you, at the moment!" laughed Len. Ruby glared at him and mouthed an indecipherable comment.

"Oh, sorry, Mr Day," continued the teacher. "My head's been in turmoil since David showed me this box you gave him."

He took a huge breath, as if to compose himself for a momentous next sentence.

"Look. There is a very big possibility that what is in here is treasure trove. This may be a collection of unfinished poems and assorted writings by William Shakespeare. If I'm right, it is worth a fortune. There are two signatures of his amongst the various letters. These alone are priceless. Did you know that only six exist in the whole world, and you've just added two more? But that isn't the best bit. David and I found, hidden in the box's lining, an ancient quill pen, and I firmly believe that it was his favourite; the one he wrote his will with."

Ruby and Len had unwittingly created a new Olympic sport called synchronized gawping. Mr Lewis continued.

"Of course, I could be talking through a small hole in the back of my neck. Until this box has been properly examined by an expert at the British Museum, what I think is of no consequence."

The Synchronized Gawpers nodded in unison.

"So, with your permission, I would like to take this box to London at the weekend for you, so that it can be examined. I have contacted a leading authority on Shakespeare, and he is eager to see me, as you can readily imagine, as soon as possible."

Lady, who had been mooching around the house, finally collapsed onto the floor by the fire and fell asleep with a huge sigh. All that Shakespeare talk can have that effect on a dog.

Len was the first to come out from under the ether. "Erm, obviously, it goes without saying, I'm delighted - overwhelmed. We both are, aren't we Rube? Bloomin' heck! I can't get it to sink in. I just keep thinking about where it came from. I paid two quid for that box from Sammy Chinn, who got it clearing an old cottage in Henley in Arden. Firstly, if it's worth anything, I ought to give him something. Then there's the old lady he got it from. See what I mean?"

"Then there's the bloke who sold her the house, and then there's the ones who sold it to them," said Mr Lewis. "You can't go beating yourself up over things like that, with great respect."

"Did you say Sammy Chinn?" asked David, as he heard a familiar name.

"Yes, he does house clearances," explained Len. "He's also a lorry driver. He delivers to my firm."

"It was someone called Chinny who was with Herbert Rhys in the fog, dad. He was the one with him the next day too, carrying the box that I thought was a coffin. He was bragging about how he took things from old ladies who never knew the value of stuff. I'm sure it would be the same man."

Mr Lewis had the look of a man listening in on a conversation in ancient Hebrew.

"Well, I wouldn't put it past him to fleece people," said Len, disgusted.

133

"Well, he didn't fleece you, Mr Day, and I wouldn't worry about rewarding him. Maybe the old lady in Henley is a different matter."

Ruby spoke up. "Maybe the box isn't worth anything. You're all counting your chickens I think. Worry about who gets what, if there's anything to get. That's what I say."

"I couldn't agree more," said Mr Lewis. "With your permission, I'll go see the professor for you. I fancy a trip to London anyway, so if it all goes belly up, it's no bother. Meanwhile, and I can't stress this strongly enough, tell no one, and don't get too excited."

At this he rose, finished his tea and called Lady. David stroked her, and she raised a paw for him to shake.

"My first bit of training!" said Mr Lewis proudly. "She likes you, David. I could see you with a nice dog." He turned to face David's parents and winked.

"Well, he does need a bit of company," admitted Len, "and something that's a bit harder to squash!"

Man, dog and box went out through the front door, and into the car.

"Bye folks," called the teacher, "and I'll be in touch after my meeting at the weekend. We'll guard this with our lives, won't we, Lady?"

The car reversed out of the *cul-de-sac*, tooted twice, and disappeared into the night.

CHAPTER 16

Third Time Unlucky

David had been past Miss Kettle's a couple of times during the week, on errands to his grandparents' house. She was back at the old stand, none the worse for her two nasty bumps to the head, or, for that matter, having to eat humble pie at the Day residence. He had thought it best to let her settle down a bit before popping in to buy his Sopwith Camel, but now, he felt, she was strong enough for him to gently re-introduce the Day motif into her life. To this end, he presented himself at the front door of the Kettle Toy and Joke Emporium, and boldly strode inside, pocket-money burning white-hot in his trousers. Had he been an Edwardian gentleman of substance, he would no doubt have been demanding of the proprietor, "Avail me of your finest plastic-moulded bi-planes and don't spare the horses, my good woman," or words to that effect, whilst slapping his gloves and cane on the counter in a debonair, devil-may-care fashion.

The quaint old shop was simply awash with Airfix's finest merchandise, aching to be purchased, but life, as David was quickly realising, was never that simple, and there was seemingly yet another hurdle to be overcome first. The shop was unmanned, or rather, unwomanned. Miss Kettle had done a bunk. She was nowhere to be seen - not amongst those present. In a word, missing.

David, who was now within touching distance of his elusive aeroplane, was not to be defeated so lightly. He employed a manoeuvre that he had twice used before, and stepped through the gap in the counter to call for Miss Kettle in the back room. Alas, she did not respond. He felt by now duty bound to inspect the floor behind the counter, and there, true to form, lay Miss Kettle, flat out under the till. As a hardened Miss Kettle observer, he should have been blasé about this latest sighting, especially as he had now seen her prostrate more often than upright. For some reason, however, he had an awful feeling creep over him as he approached her. A couple of things struck him as odd. Firstly, there was no tell-tale new bump on her brow, and crucially, the till was closed. Secondly, she was the most peculiar colour, a sort of greyish-blue. Before, her cardigan had risen and sunk slowly. This time, it was still. David was not Doctor Kildare, but he was pretty sure this time.

Miss Kettle was dead.

Gripped with panic, he left the shop, pulled the front door to and ran like fury down the hill back home with his feet hitting the pavement, on average, only once every hundred yards or so. He threw himself into the house and breathlessly alerted his mother, who ran all the way to Doctor Rodgerson's house, and luckily, found her in. A few moments later, the good doctor was in the shop, stethoscope round her neck, and examining the body. Miss Kettle, sadly, had indeed breathed her last, and had gone to the great toy shop in the sky.

David, who was not allowed in the shop, (which seemed a little over-protective as he'd seen Miss Kettle 'dead' three times already) waited in the street. Eventually the doctor and Ruby emerged, both looking a little world-weary.

"Well," boomed the doctor in her best Robertson-Justice voice, "She was a cantankerous old devil, but I don't think we'll see a character like her again in a hurry. A sad day, Mrs Day."

She locked the shop door, and returned to her surgery to summon an ambulance. Having bid farewell to the doctor, and realizing that they had done all they could, Ruby and David walked slowly and solemnly back down the high street.

"We'll have to make sure someone tells her sister in Tenbury," said Ruby, eventually.

"I don't know why I feel so sad," said David, his lip trembling. "She was really horrible to us children you know, but for some reason, I think she could have been nice, underneath. Perhaps she just needed someone to love her."

"Maybe," agreed Ruby, "but she had a funny way of showing it. She was blooming vile to us, when we were kids. She only had her sister, so it's going to be a sad funeral. Just Miss Kettle, her sister, the vicar and the bloke who plays the organ. What a send off!"

They got back home and Ruby shed her coat. There was only one thing to do after the day they'd had. She put the kettle on.

CHAPTER 17

London Calling!

Mr Lewis emerged from the underground sweating profusely, carrying a large overcoat and the old oak box in a holdall. After trudging all over London in dirty trains and sucking in the stale air of the underground tunnels, he felt as if he needed hosing down to remove the thin layer of grime he had accumulated. The wonderful frontage of the British Museum, though, was a welcome sight and helped lift his flagging spirits. Carrying such potentially precious cargo had unnerved him to the point where he felt that everyone who stood within a couple of yards of him was about to attempt a heist. His worst nightmare of leaving the blessed thing on a train had not materialized, however, and it was a relieved Dai Lewis who clumped up the front steps and in through the main doors. He asked a uniformed attendant where room one-hundred-and-eight was, and after a thousand or so more exhausting steps, he was there. He knocked gently and took a few deep breaths, to settle his pounding heart.

"Enter! Enter!" called a jolly voice from within. So he did.

Adrian Bytheway sat at his cluttered desk, looking every inch the mad professor that he was. He had a mass of thick blond hair, which gave the impression that his head had shrunk, and it was liberally curled, in the style made famous by Shirley Temple. It didn't take much imagination to see him, aged four, wearing a sailor suit and wandering around some stately grange in Oxford clutching a junior chemistry set under his arm. He wore regulation professor spectacles on the very tip of his nose and a massive and frankly garish bow tie, as popularized by Frank Muir. This ensemble was set off beautifully by a yellow tweed coat that was so loud that his neighbours complained if he wore it after eleven at night. He rose from his seat and proffered a manicured hand.

"Mr Lewis, I presume. How are you?"

Mr Lewis replied that he was well, if hot. He removed the oak box from its holdall and placed it on the table. Professor Bytheway's fingers, which had been in praying position, now began to wiggle furiously with anticipation. In an attempt, maybe subconsciously, to stall the big moment, he turned to small talk.

"Did you have a pleasant journey? Where did you say you came from? Staffordshire?"

Mr Lewis said that he was originally from Pontypridd, near Cardiff, but now lived in Brierley Bank, and had become an honorary Black Countryman.

"Ah! The Black Country. Yes indeed. Not too far from the Holy Land!"

The teacher, who was absent-mindedly toying with a life-sized plastic skull on the desk, gave the professor a look that suggested that anyone who could confuse the Black Country with Jerusalem was entirely mad. The prof decided that further explanation was necessary.

"Stratford my dear boy, Stratford upon Avon. They say Shakespeare probably spoke with an accent similar to yours."

"What, Welsh?" queried Mr Lewis.

"No, no, Black Country. Very funny. How absolute the knave is! We must speak by the card, or equivocation will undo us!"

"Osric, the fantastic fop, by any chance?" asked Mr Lewis. He understood the reference to Hamlet. Thousands of others wouldn't have, but that wouldn't have prevented the professor from using it.

"I was there recently, visiting the houses. Have you been?" the professor continued.

"Yes, many times. I was at Ann Hathaway's Cottage in the summer, but I personally prefer Mary Arden's House."

"Yes, me too. There were road-works when I went, and diversions everywhere, so I had to go Ann Hathaway!"

"Oh, very good!" smiled Mr Lewis. "Another way. Yes, excellent!" and all the time he was thinking, "Open the bloody box and tell me if it's real will you, man?"

"Tell me, Dai," asked the professor. "Have you eaten? Would you like a cup of tea?" Dai replied that he hadn't, and he would.

"Well, I'll ask Caroline, my assistant, to pop over to the pizzeria and grab a couple of pizzas. They do the most marvellous, authentic Italian stone-baked ones just across the road. It's like being in Florence. Would you like tea?"

Mr Lewis was in mental agony. He wanted a cup of tea, and he was keen enough to try a pizza, but what he really wished more than anything on God's earth was for the professor to open the blasted box and give him the blasted verdict. In his mind he could hear the audience on Michael Miles's popular quiz show shouting 'Open the bloody box.' It was as if the professor knew that this could be the greatest moment in either of their lives, and he was savouring it. Either that or he'd genuinely forgotten what his guest had come for. He picked up the internal phone, and placed an order for the food.

"Oh, excuse me, Dai, what kind of pizza do you like?" he asked, holding his hand over the mouthpiece.

Dai, ashamed of his small town ways and lack of sophistication, had to admit he'd never tasted one. The professor assured him that he'd love them, and said something patronizing about people who lived outside of London being starved of culture. He ordered a Margherita with black olives, just to be on the safe side.

"Right" said Adrian. "I can't stall this any longer. Oh my, oh my! Pass me the box, would you?"

He opened it slowly, as if it might explode in daylight. Carefully, and with great precision, he took out the various items and laid them on a second desk by the window, which was free of clutter. He stared at each piece through his spectacles, and occasionally through a magnifying glass that he produced from his coat pocket, which made him look like Sherlock Holmes. Dai half expected him to unlock a Stradivarius from a glass cabinet and light up an opium pipe, to help him think. Nothing at all was said for what seemed like an hour, but was probably only fifty-five minutes. Finally, the professor spoke.

"Gosh!" he said, just for starters. Then there was another lengthy pause.

"Well, I have waited for a moment like this all of my life, Dai. Personally, I'm convinced that these are real, but we'll need to pass them on to the handwriting experts and the paper analysts, not to mention the forensic boys and anyone else who's passing on the first floor next week. Personally - and I don't want to get your hopes up - I think it's kosher."

Mr Lewis swallowed his Adam's apple, and then tried his best to affect a nonchalant look, missing it by a mile.

"Of course, we will need your permission to hang on to all this, for a week at least. Is that okay?"

Mr Lewis said that it certainly was. He asked the professor what he thought was in the box.

"Well, Dai, there are several different types of writing. Some are house deeds and fairly uninteresting legal things. They appear to be of a later date, as if someone added to the box, not being aware of its other contents. That's probably why the house clearance bod didn't think much of his find – even very old legal deeds are two-a-penny, you see. There are letters here from other people to the Bard, which will prove fascinating in the extreme if they are judged to be real. I haven't read them yet, of course. There are poems in various stages of completion with crossings out, where a better word has been added. Priceless, my dear boy; I can't tell you! The stuff doesn't strike me as anywhere near his best, what I've read so far, but this was probably near the end of his life, and we all get a little past our best, don't we? That, however, is totally immaterial. If he had left us his shopping list, it would be worth a fortune, eh?"

Dai agreed.

"And lastly," he concluded. "This quill pen. If - and I say if - it is authentic, that and the accompanying note alone would have been more than I could have ever dreamt of. It isn't even his second-best pen, dear boy. His wife probably got left that! We've got his best one!" He slapped Mr Lewis heartily on the back. "You have made me the happiest man in London. Either that or the most disappointed, once the boffins have meddled with it. Now let's celebrate with a spot of lunch."

As he spoke, his assistant, Caroline, breezed in with two steaming boxes and a pot of tea on a large tray. She duly handed out the pizzas to their correct owners, and poured the tea into elegant china cups. Professor Bytheway opened his box and pulled off a slice. Dai, not sure of his pizza etiquette, followed the master closely. As he bit into it, he shrieked with pain.

"Oh dear!" said the professor, mortified by his guest's response to his hospitality.

"The black thing, the olive!" groaned Dai, holding his jaw.

"Oh for goodness sake!" said the prof. "How many times have I told them to remove the stones?"

Caroline spoke. She sounded as though she had plums, rather than olives, in her mouth.

"Shall I take all the olives off for you, Adrian?"

"Gosh no!" he replied. "They are to be pitted, not censured!"

Professor Bytheway's latest dubious pun was wasted on the Welshman, who was preoccupied with the searing pain that seemed to be taking over his entire skull.

The curator apologized profusely to his new acquaintance, and hoped that his first mouthful wouldn't turn him against Italian food for the rest of his life. Mr Lewis assured him that it wouldn't, and seemed rather taken with his first pizza, once his wisdom tooth had stopped aching. He observed, as they chewed contentedly, that there were no pizza restaurants in the Brierley Bank area. The professor recommended that he must move to London, but that, countered Mr Lewis, would mean he would no longer be able to buy pork scratchings, a snack that the professor had never heard of. They both eventually concluded that life was just one long compromise. After a few more slices had been consumed in silence, the professor asked Mr Lewis how he had become interested in Shakespeare.

"I studied English at Warwick University," he replied, "and got a taste for it there, I suppose."

"Well well!" smiled Adrian, "So did I! Alas poor Warwick!"

"I knew him, Horatio," added Dai, keen not to be outdone.

"A fellow of infinite jest and wisdom," continued the professor. "Who was the Dean when you were there? Michael Tooby or Peter O'Dell?"

"I must confess, I can't remember," replied Dai, spitting out a stone into his saucer."Why do you ask?"

"Tooby or not Tooby; that is the question!" chortled the professor, who clearly loved his puns, even if his quality control was somewhat lacking.

Dai wolfed down the rest of his pizza and slurped his tea. He would have loved a quick tour of the museum, but time was tight, as he needed to dash back in order to take Lady for a walk. If he didn't allow her to release her pent-up energy over Brierley Bank Park, she had a tendency to devour his settee, so he reluctantly made his excuses, blaming the awkward train connections. He thanked the pair for their hospitality, and gave them his number at the school, should there be any good news to pass on. They shook hands, and then he retraced his few thousand steps back to the front door, and out into the fresh November air.

As he walked towards the tube station, he suddenly felt compelled to jump two feet off the ground and click his heels together, much to the amusement of a passing party of Japanese tourists.

CHAPTER 18

Where There's a Will

Mr Lewis completed the register, and walked over to David's desk.

"Hello David," he beamed, "I had a nice trip down to London at the weekend, to see a colleague of mine who's mad about Shakespeare." He was speaking guardedly, because he didn't wish any of this to be public knowledge for the time being. "*Very* interesting it was too!"

He winked, and changed the subject, because the walls had ears. So too had Mally, and incredibly large ones at that. "What was all that about?" he asked, intrigued.

"I can't tell you yet," replied David, "but it could be *very* interesting."

Mally was all set to probe further, when a prefect from another class room knocked and entered, looking a little like Phidippides, the Greek runner who brought news hot-foot from the battlefield at Marathon and then keeled over.

"Sir, please sir!" gasped the red-faced child. "All the locusts have got out!"

Mr Lewis looked puzzled.

"Sir, you know they closed the science block 'cause of the subsidence, sir? Well, one of the builders has accidentally dropped the big glass box, and the locusts have escaped, sir. There were loads of them!"

Mr Lewis asked to be excused, and left Helen in charge for five minutes while he went to investigate. The room, as usual, erupted into a mass of noise and kamikaze paper aeroplane throwing. Helen had the harassed look of a female Canute, as she tried ineffectually to hold back the tide of unruliness.

"What's subsidence anyway?" asked Mally, struggling to be heard above the noise.

"Well, I suppose it's a bit like an earthquake, and the ground gives way," said David. "There are bloomin' great holes under the science block from all the old mines, my dad said."

He lifted up the lid of his desk and produced his exercise book. He added three words to his list on the back cover:

DEATH

EARTHQUAKE

PLAGUE OF LOCUSTS

Biblical Egypt had a quieter time of it than Brierley Bank was having just lately. He put the book back into his desk, and quietly endeavoured to read his Eagle comic in the midst of Bedlam.

That evening, David decided to do a spot of calligraphy, spread-eagled on the living room floor. He was a big fan of Edward Lear, and had read Lewis Carroll's 'Alice in Wonderland' and 'Alice through the Looking Glass' many times, so he thought he'd try his hand at nonsense poetry.

The best approach, he figured, was to free his mind and just see what came out. What did come out was:

Perk yourself, Monster,

This, he felt, was good stuff, and a worthy start, and he began to giggle as if demented. His mother, who was well used to such behaviour, ignored him. If he was amusing himself with something and not causing her or the people of Brierley Bank any trouble, this was okay by her. He wrote his next line.

Woblats, three a packet.

Cue more convulsions of laughter. Now he needed a rhyme.

Forty men upon a rock, Eabstove's dire racket.

Verse seemed to be flowing from him with consummate ease. Perhaps, he mused, the spirit of William Shakespeare had somehow got into him, due to handling the quill pen. He'd heard of this kind of thing happening before. David had no idea who or what Eabstove was, or why he was making a racket, let alone why the forty men were stranded on a rock, but he could hardly see to write the next two verses through his tears of laughter.

Jo Gunn, less an arm, Many are his aspirin.

This was inspired, David thought. Jo Gunn was almost certainly a pirate, and he would surely need aspirin, if he had recently lost an arm.

Radiation theory works, only when he's gaspin'.

Zebra cutlets waft a draught, who likes creosote?

By now the poor child was near apoplectic. Two lines to go and he could take a breather.

Discipline lacks all but logs, with Mrs Table-Boat.

Brilliant! His best effort to date. Now all he needed was to add a title. For some reason best known only to himself, he favoured a very long one made up of silly words. He had recently spotted a Welsh place name in his dad's map book that began with Llanfair and ran to around a million letters, whilst trying to locate Mr Weston's home town, Pontypridd, and this had left a lasting impression on him. He wrote:

Vascan-sledoogs-momomometcrongig-giglio-mothgillissie.

David knew perfection when he saw it, and wisely decided that his poem was finished, and could not be improved upon in any way. He was just about to recite it to his long-suffering mother when the door knocker clattered, and he rushed to answer it, expecting that it would be Mr Lewis with a blow-by-blow account of the London trip. Instead, there was a rather official-looking man in a gabardine mac, holding a brief case.

"Are your parents in?" he asked, so David quickly went to fetch them.

Len came to the door covered in lather, and wearing his vest. He had been endeavouring to remove a layer or two of oil and factory dust, prior to getting some smoked haddock into his system.

"Can I help you?" he asked.

"Yes, I'm from Porter, Porter and Porter, Solicitors, of Cradley Heath," said the man.

"And which one are you?" enquired Len, intrigued.

"Mr Porter," replied the man, without a hint of a smile. "May I come in for a second? I won't keep you."

Len offered him a seat, and Mr Porter opened his brief case, lifting out a slim file.

"Well," he said, "it's Master David Day that I've really come to see. Is that you?"

David was one of those children who always felt guilty when Mr Perriman accused someone of breaking a window in assembly, even when he knew full well he'd had nothing whatsoever to do with it. He was feeling guilty now. Len gave him a quick sideways glance, as if to say 'What did you do this time?'

Ruby appeared from the kitchen, smelling a little of haddock. Mr Porter, sensing a general uneasiness, continued with a comforting smile.

"No reason to worry folks. It's good news. As you know, Miss Kettle has died."

David thought this a little harsh. She wasn't to everyone's taste, but good news? Surely not.

"I'm sorry; an unfortunate way of putting it. Miss Kettle has died, and she has left a will. She wasn't a massively wealthy woman, but by no means a pauper either. She'd run that toy shop for many years, and had no expenses to speak of. No husband, no children, just a sister in Tenbury who had never needed any financial help. No, she quietly did okay thank you very much." He opened his file, and produced her last will and testament. "It appears folks, that she changed her will shortly before she died, and guess who she included in it?" He looked at David, and smiled.

"We did about wills at school," said David. "Shakespeare left his wife an old bed!"

"Well, Miss Kettle has left you something better than an old bed, son. She's left you five hundred pounds!"

The Day family looked at each other in blank amazement, and not for the first time. Five hundred pounds was an incredible amount, especially for a lad she didn't even know. They said as much to Mr Porter.

"She told us that you had been kind to her, and tried to bring her round after she banged her head. She also said that she felt guilty, accusing you of robbing her and whacking her with a cricket bat. Miss Kettle never had children, you see, and it made her a little bitter and resentful, according to her sister. Anyway, she's left you a lot of money, son, and it's my pleasure to hand over this cheque, and then I'll be on my way. Someone's got haddock, and I don't want to get in the way at teatime."

He got up, put on his mac and shook hands with David and his parents, who escorted him to the door, thanking him profusely. This really was a turn up for the books. Returning to the living room, they congratulated David, who was scrutinizing the cheque (with a view to possibly forging it at some later date with his thirteen-colour biro), and looking very thoughtful.

"It's her funeral soon, isn't it?" he said to his mother.

"Yes, on Wednesday, at four o clock, I think."

"Who'll be at it?" he asked.

"Well, we ought to go, especially now," she said. "Her sister will be there too, and the vicar, and the man who plays the organ. I can't imagine anyone else going, David. I'm afraid she wasn't very popular. She was very grumpy, after all."

David continued to look thoughtful. He was dangerous when he was like this. Luckily, the door knocker clattered again, so he went to answer it while Ruby finished serving the haddock. Len looked heavenward, and offered a silent prayer to God to let him eat his food, just one night, without interruption.

Mr Lewis came into the room grinning broadly. His expression changed to apologetic when he saw the dinner being placed on the table. He volunteered to return shortly, but Len beckoned him to sit down and asked him if he wanted tea. The teacher said that tea would be lovely, so Len asked Ruby to make some. He was a good man, but he'd been brought up that way, and in fairness, she did the same to him, when a shelf needed putting up.

As Len digested his haddock in huge, unchewed lumps, Dai began relating his London experiences. Everyone was bucked by the news, but they kept reminding themselves that nothing was certain till the forensic boys had done their bit.

"I'll believe it when I see it," said Ruby. "I've had too many disappointments in the past."

"Sir?" said David.

"Yes David?" replied sir.

"I've got an idea. You know - if these Shakespeare things are real - we'll make a lot of money?"

"Not me, David, but you, yes."

"If I made a lot of money sir, I'd give you some, of course!"

Both parents quickly endorsed this.

"No, no. It's not necessary," insisted the honest fellow, quietly thinking that the cost of a return London train ticket might be nice, however.

"Yes, I *will* give you some, sir," David assured him. He continued. "Anyway, sir, if it made me a lot of money, I wouldn't need *this* money, would I?" He showed his teacher the cheque, and explained how he'd come by it.

Mr Lewis couldn't see where this was going. Len, knowing David, already had an inkling.

"Well, sir, I want to do something nice for Miss Kettle, you see. I don't think anyone will go to her funeral, because she was a bit crabby and bad tempered. I've been thinking about it, and it seems ever so sad, an empty church."

Mr Lewis said he knew about Miss Kettle's death, and he agreed that; A, It was sad, and B, Yes, she was a crabby old thing. He'd gone into her shop recently and she'd bitten his head off for no apparent reason, other than ringing her blasted bell.

"Well, sir, I've had a good idea. I want all the children from school to go to her funeral."

Mr Lewis agreed that it was a lovely idea, but doubted that the children would be keen to go of their own free will. For a start, nobody liked funerals, and secondly, nobody liked Miss Kettle. David explained that he had thought of a plan, to get them all to agree to go.

"What if we had a Christmas party for the whole school, with jelly, cakes, games and crackers, but the children could only go if they promised to turn up at the church on Wednesday at four o clock first?" asked David.

"Nice idea, David," said Mr Lewis, "but Mr Perriman just wouldn't allow it. He'd agree to sending the children during lesson time, I'm sure, but if the funeral is after school hours, we can't dictate that children go anywhere they don't want to. Also, we simply don't have the money!"

"No, but I do!" said David, waving his new cheque at the assembled cast. "I want to spend this money on a party for all of us, with one condition. You don't turn up on Wednesday; you don't come to the party."

Not for the first time, Len and Ruby raised their eyes to heaven. Mr Lewis was just about to offer a spirited argument.

"Don't bother, Mr Lewis. He's made his mind up. We've learnt not to argue," said Len, taking his plate back into the kitchen.

CHAPTER 19

Alas, Poor Kettle

Brierley Bank Church was full to overflowing. Only the upper school had been asked to attend, because teachers were a little worried about the younger children being disturbed by the coffin and the solemnity of the occasion. The Christmas party bribe had been announced in assembly, once Mr Perriman had skilfully reconstructed David's original idea. It wasn't the best thought-out plan to tell the assembled multitude that, unless they attended a funeral, they couldn't go to a party, well-meant though it was. He subtly adapted the phrasing so that Miss Kettle herself had donated the money to the school, and naturally Mr Perriman expected, in return, for his flock to offer their condolences.

This had rather taken the limelight off David. After all, it was *his* five hundred pounds, not the school's, but after sensitive discussions involving David, his parents, the Head and Mr Lewis, all agreed that this was the best way. Mr Perriman also agreed to meet David half-way with funding, ensuring the lad still ended up with a tidy sum in his building society account. After all, the school, thought its Head, needed cheering up that particular Christmas. A spoonful of sugar to help the medicine go down.

There were precious few conscientious objectors. Presumably, not even a ton of jelly and ice cream would entice these hardened characters to a funeral, especially Miss Kettle's. Maybe they had felt the wrath of her tongue once too often, and could not forgive. Perhaps they were clever enough to realize that they'd probably get invited to the party anyway. Whatever their reasons, they must have numbered no more than a handful.

The pews were packed and it was standing room only at the back. Most, at the tender age of eleven or less, had never been to a funeral and were a little apprehensive about what went on. The vicar had been advised to make it as joyous an affair as was humanly possible, given the average age of the clientele. He did his best, under the circumstances, but funerals had to have coffins, he explained. It was traditional.

The air of foreboding wasn't helped by certain members of David's class, who kept whispering to each other about the lid shooting off and a zombified Miss Kettle rising from the dead to chase them away, as she had often done in life. This silly nonsense spread with forest fire rapidity, until virtually all the eyes in the room were intently focused on the oak casket instead of the vicar. The unwelcome distraction seemed to rattle the normally unflappable cleric and caused him to occasionally lose the thread, which resulted in what could best be described as a less than confident performance. He eventually interrupted his sermon to respectfully request that the congregation must only have eyes for him during the rest of the service, and they begrudgingly conformed.

A few hymns were sung, and the event was no more or less boring than the average end of term carol service, once the children had forgotten about the dead body in their midst.

Everyone was fairly cheerful, because no one knew the woman well enough to get upset. Only one lady on the front row, unnoticed by most of the room, shed copious tears. It would have been rather nice to think that half of her tears were of grief for a lost sister, and the other half, tears of pride, after seeing how many of the town's children had thought enough of Miss Kettle to pack the church to capacity.

The vicar said a few kind words about the deceased, but he was clearly struggling to make a whole paragraph. He recited the Lord's Prayer, and all the children joined in. Mr Lewis, by far the best choice for a reading, with his rich, Welsh tones, rose from his seat and took his place at the lectern. He opened a well-thumbed book, and read.

Fear no more the heat o' the sun.

Nor the furious winter's rages;

Thou thy worldly task hast done,

Home art gone, and ta'en thy wages:

Golden lads and girls all must,

As chimney sweepers, come to dust.

Fear no more the frown o' the great,

Thou art past the tyrant's stroke;

Care no more to clothe, and eat;

To thee the reed is as the oak:

The sceptre, learning, physic must

All follow this, and come to dust.

He quietly removed his reading glasses, and sat down. The organist began to play a solemn dirge, and the curtain drew across the coffin, much to the relief of a few hundred children, who would no doubt dream terrible dreams that night, all for the chance to get sick on jelly and play pass the parcel sometime in December. One more hymn, a spirited rendition of 'All Things Bright and Beautiful' and the funeral was over. The children flooded out of the church to be met by the parents who hadn't chosen to attend, and everyone made their way home. Mr Lewis called to David and his parents on the way out.

"Hello, Mr and Mrs Day. I just thought I'd tell you, as if you didn't know already, what a great little lad you have here. All this was down to him. Can you imagine what a dismal affair it would have been without his efforts?"

He ruffled up David's hair, much to the boy's annoyance. He forgave Mr Lewis, as he was his favourite teacher, but the next one to do it was in danger of having his shins kicked senseless. Ruby and Len gave David a hug, which caused him to blush bright red and say 'Gerroff!' Mr Lewis reminded them that the results of the British Museum tests would be with them by the end of the week. He also advised them not to tell anyone about what was going on.

"You can't be too careful," he warned. "If anyone gets wind of it, you could be causing yourself a lot of trouble." He ran a hand through David's hair once more and walked off to his car.

CHAPTER 20

A Game of Pass the Parcel

It was eight-thirty on Saturday morning, and Len was making a cup of tea in the kitchen. Ruby was still in bed, having a well-earned lie in. Usually, he worked on Saturday mornings until midday, but he had taken a weekend off to catch up on some domestic chores, namely, the building of three pinewood shelves for David's bedroom. He was just about to take Ruby a cup of tea in bed when the door knocker clattered. Still in pyjamas, he opened the door to find a man in a blue shirt and tie, with the words SECURITY UK embroidered on his breast pocket. He was wearing a large, black motorcycle-style helmet.

"Morning, mate!" he said gruffly, "Sign here, here, here, and here."

Len signed there, there, there, and finally there, as he was told. The gruff man handed him a large padded brown paper package, with SECURITY UK stickers all over it. He also handed him a letter, addressed to 'David Day and family. Private and Confidential.' Len thanked the man, and closed the door. He laid the package down on the breakfast table and opened the letter. He could guess what the package was.

What he really needed to see in a hurry was the response from the British Museum. David was fast asleep in bed, and Len didn't feel too guilty, as the letter was clearly addressed to all of them. He read:

Dear David and Family,

Please find enclosed your oak box and its contents. We think it best that they are safely returned to you until you decide their future. Can I advise that the contents should be kept somewhere secure, as we have some wonderful news for you.

After much forensic testing, handwriting analysis and expert scrutiny, we are convinced that, with the exception of a few deeds and legal documents, (which are in themselves of much interest) the contents of the box, and the box itself, are without doubt the original property and writings of William Shakespeare.

I hardly need tell you the importance of such a find, and obviously, we at the British Museum would wish to keep these wonderful artefacts in England. This one box alone has added to our total number if authenticated signatures by a third!

The quill pen, without any of the poems and writings, would fetch untold amounts at auction. Obviously, you are within your rights to keep the items, or sell them to whomsoever you wish. I would, however, personally appeal to you to carefully consider where these national treasures will end up. It would be a tragedy of Shakespearian proportion if they were to end up in America, for example.

To this end, The British Museum has agreed to pay you the sum of two hundred and fifty thousand pounds in cash, to secure the box for the nation. It is only fair to point out that several private bidders could exceed that amount at auction, but our budget is limited. The figure mentioned is our final offer, and is frankly stretching us to the limit!

Please take your time to consider this carefully, and feel free to ring, or write to me, Professor Adrian Bytheway, at the above address.

May I also ask you to thank Mr Dai Lewis for all his help in this matter? I'm sure you'll agree that without his keen eye, none of this would have come to light.

I look forward to hearing from you.

Yours sincerely,

Professor Adrian Bytheway.

Len felt dizzy. He'd read the letter but it didn't sink in, and he had to clutch the breakfast bar to stop himself falling over. He could see two letters, dancing in unison before his eyes. Pulling himself together with a huge mental effort, he grabbed the tea tray and staggered upstairs. Seeing Ruby snoring peacefully, he hadn't the heart to wake her. He polished off her tea, got himself dressed, and popped down to the sanctity of his garden shed, where he could get to grips with the contents of the letter and its consequences, whilst sawing his pinewood planks.

* * *

Sammy Chinn, that astute businessman and entrepreneur, blissfully unaware that he had sold gullible old Len a boxful of priceless artefacts for two quid, was calling on Len's place of work at nine-thirty, Saturday morning, to show him his latest acquisition, a flintlock pistol.

Imagine his disappointment then, when Jack Tromans, Len's friend and fellow tool-maker, informed him of Len's day off. Unperturbed, Sammy decided to take a small detour on his way back to Aston and call by the Day residence, in order to show him and his son the rather beautiful weapon, which he'd somehow managed to purchase for a pittance from a ninety-two-year-old retired sea captain from Stow on the Wold, as part of a house clearance. He was not driving the lorry that day, and had elected to use his own beaten-up van to drop off some metal sheeting. This was not some altruistic gesture to save his firm some petrol money. It was because, *en-route* to Len's factory, he had to pick up a Staffordshire bull terrier bitch from a man in Quinton, for breeding purposes. His original client, against his better judgment, had been patient after the previous debacle, because Sammy had promised to supply a replacement bitch within a week or two. This animal, which was marginally more relaxed about Sammy taking her on a mystery tour than the previous one had been, lay peacefully in the back of the van, chewing on an old oily rag.

Sammy pulled up in the small *cul-de-sac* and went to the outhouse door which led directly to the kitchen. He had been to Len's place before, so he knew the layout well. He gently tapped the door, but no one answered, so he opened it and popped his head inside.

"Len! Mrs Day! Anyone about?" he called, but no one appeared to be at home. He wandered in, and was about to shout upstairs when he saw a large package, marked SECURITY UK on the table, with a letter from the British Museum. Sammy, being Sammy, began to read the letter, as he helped himself to the half a round of toast that Len had left. When he got about halfway down the page, his eyes nearly popped from their sockets. Hands trembling, he quickly examined the contents of the opened packaging.

"The bloody sods!" he said, teeth gritted and face like thunder. Grabbing the package and checking to make sure that he hadn't been seen, he made for the door, and was away in seconds. He threw the package onto the passenger seat, reversed out of the *cul-de-sac* and drove back in the direction of Birmingham, his mind racing. No one had seen him, and no one would suspect him. He was going to be a very rich man. All he needed was someone to fence the goods. These were no ordinary antiques; they were priceless treasures, and he'd let them go for two quid! He vowed to be a damned sight more careful in future.

What he needed was a contact in America. They were crazy about Shakespeare there, and they'd pay the top dollar. It was feasible that he could make three hundred grand, maybe more. He was so excited, he almost forgot about his appointment with a stud dog in Cradley Heath. Trying desperately to put a lid on his emotions, he headed there now. Sammy was feeling aggrieved that he had to channel his energies into mating this blasted dog in order to earn a few paltry pounds, when vast fortunes beckoned. What was once a nice little money earner had now become a nuisance. That said, it would inevitably take a considerable time to complete such a complex deal with the Americans, and he did need immediate funds. Reeling in his impatient streak, he reconciled himself to the task ahead, and pulled his rusting van into the petrol station.

He was on empty. Another mile and the van would have ground to a halt. The kiosk attendant came out and began filling the tank while Sammy went into the little shop to buy a pork pie, a bottle of Tizer and some cigarettes. Here was a man who understood that his body was his temple, albeit a ruined one. He reached up high on the top shelf for a magazine which catered for lonely men, because he needed some intellectual stimulation while he ate his snack. Presently, the young man returned to his kiosk, and totted up Sammy's bill.

"That's a pork pie, a packet of Woodbines and the Tizer," said the lad, and took Sammy's money. Sammy thanked him, and walked out of the shop. When he was clear, he removed the magazine from his sheepskin coat, and headed for the concrete bench situated on a small strip of grass next to the garage. He had ten minutes before he was expected in Cradley Heath, and all this dreaming of untold wealth had made him peckish. Sammy polished off the pork pie, gulped the Tizer down, and then lit a thoughtful fag. Within a week or two, he could be incredibly rich. No more mating dogs for a few quid, no more house clearances, and definitely no more delivering filthy sheets of steel. With money like that, he could retire. He let fly with a revolting pork pie-tainted belch, rose to his feet, and returned to his van.

The Staffordshire bull terrier seemed pleased to see him. She had been a bit lonely, for this is a breed that craves human company, even if it's in the odious form of Sammy Chinn. She was also a mite peckish, having not eaten all day. It was possibly because of this that she had chewed the contents of his Security UK package into a thousand small, soggy pieces.

CHAPTER 21

Love's Labours Lost

Len had successfully sawn out his shelves, sanded the edges for a professional finish, and now felt the need for a nice cup of tea. He was always feeling the need for a nice cup of tea, though he was forever telling anyone who'd listen that it tasted awful just lately, and he was going off it. He'd been saying that for thirty years, and yet he always drank around fifteen cups a day. Still, it was better than being addicted to Woodbines and it was considerably more sociable. He was about to pick up his teacup from the breakfast table where he'd left it, when he noticed that the package was missing. He did not immediately panic, because he presumed that David might have moved it. He looked in the living room, and called upstairs, but David had obviously gone out, presumably to see Mally.

He searched the house, but the package was nowhere to be seen. David wouldn't have taken it out with him; he knew how shrouded in secrecy this was. Len was beginning to panic now, and beads of sweat were forming on his brow. Where on earth could it be? He called upstairs to Ruby, who was in the bathroom, and asked her if she'd seen it. She replied that she hadn't even been downstairs yet, let alone seen a package. The world began to swim before Len's eyes.

Then he noticed the plate, where his toast had been, and he knew that he wasn't losing his marbles. He had definitely left a piece of toast there because it was too burnt. He hated burnt toast, as did David. If he hadn't eaten it, and David hadn't, who had? Ruby, by her own admission, had not even been downstairs yet. It was dawning on Len, with sickening certainty, that he had been burgled, and by a hungry thief. He felt so faint that he slumped into a chair and could not move for what seemed like an age. He had been within a thousandth of an inch of securing a life of luxury for himself and his family, and he – yes, he personally - had thrown it all away by not locking the outhouse door. The British Museum had expressly asked him to put the contents in a safe place, and instead, he had sauntered down to the shed to make shelves, and ruined everything for the ones he loved. A horrible feeling of pity and self-loathing engulfed him, and he began to sob quietly. He had only ever felt this awful once before.

When David was a tiny baby, the dreaded Asian flu was sweeping across England, and thousands of people, particularly the very young and the very old, were dying of it. Ruby was in bed with the virus, extremely ill, and David was in a critical condition. The doctor was concerned and had visited the house several times, and Len was having to do the cooking, cleaning and ironing, as well as doing a gruelling full day in the factory, once Bertha had arrived to take over. One evening, after he had done a load of washing, which was left drying on two clotheshorses by the fire, he checked on his poorly wife and child, and thankfully, found them both sleeping peacefully. He returned downstairs and opened a bottle of stout. This was the only time he'd had to rest for two weeks, and his eyes were heavy. He made himself a cheese sandwich, and spread out in the comfy armchair by the fire.

Just as he put the glass to his mouth, there was a mighty whooshing noise, and suddenly around a ton of soot came down the chimney and totally engulfed the room. The clothes, the walls, the floor, the sandwich, the beer and Len all went black. He said nothing, for here was a man who had never uttered a swear-word in his life. He just sobbed quietly, much as he was doing right now. Once he had regained his composure and reminded himself that he was a man, he meekly made a pot of tea and took it upstairs. For years afterwards, Ruby was convinced that she had become delirious with the flu, and imagined that Al Jolson had bought her tea in bed.

Strangely, this current outpouring of emotion had done him the world of good, and his brain began to think a little more clearly. He put on his coat and walked down to the phone box just across the street. Clutching a small piece of paper in one hand, and tucking the receiver under his chin, he began to dial the number. Mr Lewis was out in the garden, trying in vain to educate his new dog in the art of stick retrieval, when he heard the phone ringing. He dashed up the garden path and picked up the receiver, breathing heavily, like a dirty caller.

"Hello?"

"Oh, hello Mr Lewis, Len Day here. There's a bit of a problem and I need advice. Any chance of popping round?"

Dai Lewis said that there was, and reached for his coat.

* * *

David was out with Mally, walking over Casson's Wood. They paused for a rest by a huge old oak tree, so that Mally could try to spot the Tree Creeper he'd seen the week before.

"Dave," he said, after a considerable silence. "Are you worried about this exam?"

David said that he was, because it was going to make a big difference to their lives. His dad had said that he thought it was wrong to sort children into two piles at the age of eleven. 'One lot go to the rubbish school and the factory; one lot to the good school and the posh jobs', was how he'd phrased it. His dad also said that he knew people who were completely brainless that had passed for Grammar school, and people that were very bright who'd ended up in filthy dead-end jobs. He, after all, should know.

"It's okay for you, Dave," sighed Mally. "Everyone knows you're a brainbox. You're good at art and music and writing and stuff. You'll pass it no trouble. I'm hopeless at maths and English, and nearly everything else, come to think about it. I'm only good at country stuff, like bird-watching and taxidermy."

"I'm rubbish at maths too," confided David, trying to put his friend at ease. "When they ask me how many times a man needs to fill his wheelbarrow to empty a three-yard-square hole in a field, I don't have a clue what they're on about!"

"If I was to fail, and you was to pass, would you go to the Secondary School with me, so that we could still be mates?" asked Mally, hopefully.

"But you *will* pass, Mal, trust me," David assured him, skilfully side-stepping the question. "Then you can go to Grammar school with me. That's if *I* pass! You might pass, and I might fail. Would you come to the Secondary School with me then?"

"Yeah, course," said Mally, with all the selfless attitude of a boy that knew in his heart of hearts that passing would be a struggle. This awkward conversation was the first time the two friends had broached the subject.

"Anyway, whatever happens, we can still be friends. Even if we go to different schools," David assured him. "We aren't moving house you know!"

"Course!" said Mally, far from convinced. In Brierley Bank, the Senior Slugs seldom spoke to Grammar Grubs.

They stood up, dusted off their trousers, and walked back towards home. Mally said goodbye at his front gate, and David headed for his house to continue with his calligraphy. He was planning a bit of a surprise for Mr Lewis, and couldn't wait to get on with it. He breezed into the kitchen to find the eventual recipient of his surprise talking to his Dad, over a cup of tea. They looked extremely subdued.

"Oh, hello, sir!" he said. "Hello, dad."

"Hello David," sighed Len. "Er, David, did you see the great big padded brown package on the table, and a letter?"

"Yes," replied David.

"And did you read the letter, by any chance?" said Len.

"No, I was going to, but I went to see Mally."

"You haven't, you know, moved that envelope have you? Was it there when you went out to play?" asked Len.

"Yes, it was definitely there, dad; and the letter," said David. "What's up?"

"Oh, er, nothing really. Your mom has probably been tidying up, that's all," said Len, glancing at Dai.

"I wouldn't think so," replied David. "Mom's been in bed all morning. She didn't look too well when I went in earlier. She said she'd be okay if she had a bit more sleep."

Len had to confess that, with one thing and another, he hadn't realized that his wife was feeling a bit under the weather. His mind flashed back to the terrible flu incident, and a look of panic crossed his face. At that precise moment, Ruby emerged, clad in dressing gown, and greeted them.

"I'm okay," she smiled. "I just felt a bit rough for some reason. Alright now though. Probably a dodgy haddock!"

She poured herself a cup of tea, and being an intuitive soul, realized straight away that all was not well. She looked towards Len with a pleading expression, but he put a quick finger to his lips.

"David," said Mr Lewis. "You haven't told anyone about our secret have you? Mally, or anyone at the school?" David replied that he definitely hadn't, even though it was killing him to keep quiet.

"Anyway," said David, "What's going on? Is there a problem?"

At that moment the outhouse door burst open, and in came Jack Tromans in his brown cow-gown, carrying six steel brackets.

"Mornin' Len. Mornin' all!" he bellowed, at a volume that was just short of ear-shattering. "Just thought I'd drop off your brackets for the bedroom shelves, mate. They look alright don't they?"

Len agreed that he'd done a good job. When work was a little slack, the men would occasionally employ their skills on what were known as 'foreigners'. It seemed a shame to have the cream of the Black Country standing idle, when there were shelf brackets needed in bedrooms.

Len had asked his lifelong pal, Jack, to help him out while he took the day off. A task he was only too pleased to assist with, as his foreman was very good to him, and turned a blind eye when he constructed his fish tank during dinner breaks, using the firm's steel. Len was propriety itself, but after a whole lifetime with nothing more than a cheap gold watch to show for his efforts, he figured that a huge firm could donate the odd shelf bracket. Jack handed over his handiwork and said thanks, but no thanks; he didn't want any tea, as it was swilling around up to his tonsils already. As he turned to go, he spoke to David.

"What do you think of that flintlock then, Dave? Wasn't it a beauty?"

David gave him the look that suggested Jack had taken him into dark and unfathomed waters. He had the air of a boy who did not get the gist.

"What flintlock?" he asked, puzzled.

"Oh, didn't he bring it after all? Sammy Chinn was at the works this morning, and he'd got a cracking flintlock pistol for sale. He knows that Len's favourite film was 'Treasure Island', with Robert Newton, and he's always had a thing about flintlocks, haven't you, Len? Sammy wondered if young David might like it. He said he'd call round your place this morning. Perhaps he was running late with a delivery. Any road, he'll be in later in the week. I daresay he'll still have it."

With this, Jack bade them farewell and exited stage-right, shutting the door so hard that Mr Lewis leapt from his kitchen stool. Len gave Dai another telling look. The cogs were whirring in his brain. He had put two and two together, and got the arithmetic spot on.

"Sammy Chinn!" he said through gritted teeth. "There's your man." He explained to a lost-looking Mr Lewis that he was the original seller of the items in question, and though, on the surface he was a cheeky, grinning, affable Brummie, he wouldn't trust him as far as he could chuck him. Mr Lewis's hands curled into fists, and he whacked the edge of the table, causing Len's umpteenth cup of tea to spill into the saucer.

"Smiling, damned villain!" he snarled, but the quote from Hamlet was totally lost on those present. Ruby, who had come into this rather late, was giving Len a quizzical look. David, equally perplexed, asked, "Dad, what's going on? Has something happened?"

Len stood up. There was no easy way to say this, so he came straight out with it.

"There's been a problem. The stuff came back from London early today, with this letter. The museum has agreed to pay us an incredible amount for them. Two hundred and fifty thousand pounds, to be precise. A quarter of a million."

Mr Lewis nearly fell off his stool for the second time in a minute. David and Ruby just gawped at each other.

"*How* much?" they sang, in ragged three-part harmony, with Dai's rich baritone voice taking bottom C, Ruby the E and David the top G.

"Yes, a blooming fortune. They sent the stuff back for safe keeping, to give us time to chew it over, as if we needed it! I went down the shed to make my shelves, and in this time, we now suspect that Sammy Chinn, who sold us the stuff in the first place, came in, presumably to show us this flintlock, saw the letter and realized that he'd been well and truly done. He must have then taken the box, and I bet you that right now, he's negotiating with some auction house or other to see if can get even more than two hundred and fifty thousand. Whatever he negotiates, it'll be a bit better than the two quid he got from me. The worst thing is, we'd have a hell of a game trying to prove he stole it!"

David weighed this, and spoke. He couldn't grasp one particular aspect of this tale.

"Dad, I get all that, but how did Sammy Chinn know where to look for the box?"

Len looked equally puzzled. "Well I just explained, David. He came in through the door, found no one about, grabbed the brown padded envelope off the table and scarpered".

"Yes" said David impatiently, "But how did he know the box was under my bed?"

Len, now exasperated, replied. "The box wasn't under your bed, it was in the envelope!"

"No," explained David. "When I saw the envelope this morning, I got the box out and put it back under my bed, for safe keeping, like the museum told us to. Then, rather than waste that nice big envelope, I put all my calligraphy forgeries in there, because I was going to give them to Mr Lewis for a present on Monday, to say thank you for all his help. I've copied most of those documents and letters and stuff with my calligraphy pens and I was just about to start on the last couple. It took me ages, and now it looks like they've all gone!"

Mr Lewis looked at Len. Len looked at Mr Lewis. Ruby looked alternately at both of them. Very slowly, huge smiles appeared on all of their faces.

"Pop up to your room, David, and get me the box. There's a good lad," said Len.

"Yes boyo. Fast as you like!" added Mr Lewis.

David was back with the box within seconds. Everything was intact. Three adults began to breathe once more, and the sense of relief in the room was palpable. As the kettle was filling, and the celebratory biscuits arriving on a plate, Mr Lewis chuckled.

"I'd love to be a fly on the wall when Sammy gets those documents out of his briefcase in some swish hotel in London, with a couple of posh auction house directors in pinstriped suits and bow ties, looking all hopeful."

They all laughed loudly.

"He'll be a laughing stock!" said Ruby.

"I hope they beat him senseless for wasting their time, and tear the stuff up in front of his eyes!" said Len, who was showing an unusually ruthless side.

"Well I don't think it's very funny!" interjected David. "I spent all week doing those, and now they've all been nicked!"

Mr Lewis put his arm around him and said something about it being the thought that counted. This seemed to pacify the boy just a little. Maybe, if Interpol did catch up with Chinny, he reasoned, they may be able to return the goods.

They all agreed, not realizing that, as they spoke, the goods were being messily recycled in Quinton Park by a pregnant bitch.

CHAPTER 22

A Nasty Bump on the Head

Len was talking to Jack Tromans when Sammy Chinn arrived, carrying a cardboard box.

"Hello Len, hello Jack," he mumbled.

Len wasn't sure if Sammy had a sheepish, guilty look, or if he had merely read that into his expression because he knew what he'd been up to. It was certainly true that the normally matey Sammy was sounding a little more strained and formal than in previous weeks, as if something was eating at him. It was thus that these two prize-fighters weighed each other, neither wishing to make the first move that could end in disaster.

"I've got something here that your lad might like," said Sammy, getting down to business.

"Ah, the flintlock!" said Jack. "I thought you said you were dropping round to Len's place on Saturday with that."

Sammy looked decidedly flustered upon hearing Jack's comment. "Oh, yeah! I was, erm, running a bit late, so I didn't go."

"That's what I suspected, wasn't it Len?"

Len said yes. His eyes were glazed over, and he continued to file a piece of steel as nonchalantly as he could. Sammy produced the weapon and gave it to Len. It was a lovely thing, and it spoke to Len's depths. He examined it carefully, and pulled back the hammer. In spite of its age, it snapped down beautifully. Len appreciated craftsmanship in wood and metal, and since he was David's age, he had been fascinated by the romance of the eighteenth century; especially smugglers, galleons and flintlock pistols. Sammy, who was gaining confidence with every sentence, was now sure that Len knew nothing. After all, he was examining the gun with interest and behaving normally. No, everything was okay, though Jack's earlier comment about visiting the house had been unnerving. Still, no real harm done, but he was still livid with Len for making such an obscene profit from one of their transactions. Sammy could never have done that to anyone. It was a sneaky trick.

"Look at that brass ball on the end of the butt," said Sammy, lightening the tone. "The engraving is beautiful. You don't get craftsmanship like that nowadays, eh Len?"

Len agreed.

Jack chipped in. "It wasn't just decorative either. Because these guns only had one shot, and they were a bugger to reload, so they could use that end to club their enemy, when they got close enough!"

Len was interested in this.

"Like this?" he asked, suddenly swinging the gun back and catching Sammy with a fearful blow to the brow. Sammy buckled instantly, and with a groan, slumped to the floor in a heap. A huge red weal had appeared, and his eyes had lost their focus. Curiously, bumps on the head were fast becoming a sort of *leitmotif* in the David's world. It was almost as if they had become the latest fashion, and suddenly everybody wanted to sport one.

Cassius Clay experienced a very similar sensation to Sammy's, whilst chattering away to Henry Cooper during their famous World Championship encounter. One minute the pair seemed to be getting on famously, and the next, Henry was punching Cassius Clay's lights out, which, it has to be said, was against the general consensus at bookmaker's shops up and down the land. The whole incident seemed to go completely against the run of play, and this is exactly how Jack Tromans felt *vis-à-vis* the Len and Sammy affair, as he watched the drama unfold.

In fairness to Cassius Clay, seconds after his unexpected setback, he was quickly on his feet again and gaining the upper hand. Sammy though, didn't seem in good enough shape to do likewise, and appeared to be taking an impromptu nap on the dirty tool-room floor. Jack stood goggle-eyed with wonder, his eyes darting nervously betwixt the slayer and the slain. He hadn't the foggiest what had brought this on, and from Len, of all people, that mildest of mild-mannered gentlemen.

"That's for eating my toast!" snarled Len cryptically at the comatose Sammy.

Jack made a mental note never to borrow an apple from Len's lunch box ever again.

Sammy eventually came to in the back of his van, around five minutes later. Len was slapping his face, not so much in an effort to encourage him to regain consciousness, but more to satisfy an overwhelming desire to hit him again. One eye opened, and stared at his slayer. Len, who had taken Sergeant Rhys's correspondence course in 'The criminal classes and how to best deal with them,' spoke softly and carried a big stick, both literally and metaphorically.

"Ah, Sammy, so nice to have you with us once more," he spat."Don't say a word; don't spoil this cherished moment together. Just listen. I know that you broke into my house, and stole what didn't belong to you. Correct?"

Sammy nodded.

"I could easily have told Sergeant Rhys, and he'd have fingerprinted the outhouse door, and probably waited for my toast to emerge from the other end of you so he could take it away for examination. You could have been looking at six months. I chose to mete out my own version of justice instead. Okay with you?"

Sammy nodded again.

"Now listen, I'll keep the gun for my lad, free of charge, we'll forget all about the breaking and entering. You'll continue to deliver my steel, and we'll bid each other a pleasant 'good morning' as before, but there'll be no more antiques and goods robbed from old ladies. That fine with you?"

Sammy said that it was, but he wished to add something. Len, like Mally, was all ears. A feeble voice croaked its pitiful message.

"S-S-Sorry Len. There's something I've got to tell you, and I don't want to be hit no more, okay?"

Len agreed.

"Promise? It's not good news, Len."

Len promised. His fingers were crossed behind his back, just in case.

"It's the documents. You're not going to like this, Len. They were eaten by a dog."

Sammy winced, and waited for the next blow. None came. He thought, just for a second, that he even saw a wry smile on Len's lips.

"That's a great shame," said Len. "They meant a lot to my son."

"But Len, what about all that money?" said Sammy, incredulously.

"Well, it's a blow, I can't deny it," replied Len, hamming it up terribly. "But perhaps it's for the best. Two hundred and fifty grand could destroy my family. We might not know how to handle it. We could turn to drink or drugs even. We could spend, spend, spend and end up destitute. I was once told about a boxer who spent most of his fortune on women, booze and drugs, Sammy. When he was asked what he'd done with the rest, he said he'd just wasted it. I don't want that kind of life. No, on reflection, it's probably all for the best, Sammy. All for the best."

Len backed out of the open doors of the van, leaving Sammy mentally, as well as physically, stunned. The driver had expected a savage beating with a metal shelf bracket, or at least a screaming match, but none had come. He rose shakily to his feet, and feeling that, all things considered, he had got away lightly, he slumped behind the steering wheel and headed back to Aston, a broken man.

"Hard but fair!" he mused, as he tried desperately to negotiate Old Hill traffic island with double vision. "Hard but fair!"

180

CHAPTER 23

Miss Kettle is Dead - Long Live Miss Kettle!

Ruby was at the kitchen table, biro in hand, for she was the neater writer of the two. Len, who was the better dictator, stood behind her, dictating.

Dear Professor Bytheway,

Thank you for your letter and extremely generous offer. The money is most welcome and will change our lives. We have no intention of trying to better the offer by going to private auctions. Also, we wish the treasures to remain in Britain to be enjoyed by Shakespeare's own people, in your Museum.

I trust you will arrange for the items to be picked up soon. We are a bit nervous about having them here, as you can imagine.

Yours Sincerely,

Len, Ruby and David Day.

P.S. When can we have the money? Just before Christmas would be nice.

The letter was posted on Tuesday morning, and on the following Friday there was a knock on the front door. It was the gruff, helmeted character from Security UK once more, asking Ruby this time, to sign on the dotted line. He collected the precious oak box and handed her a white envelope, marked David Day and Family - Private and Confidential. He placed the box carefully into the back of his van and was gone. She opened the envelope and removed the letter. It read;

Dear David and Family,

Thank you for agreeing to sell the Shakespeare items to the British Museum. Too often have such treasures disappeared abroad, so it's refreshing to find a family that isn't at all greedy, and has the welfare of the country at heart.

I have enclosed an initial cheque for a hundred and twenty-five thousand pounds as a deposit. You will receive a further cheque for the balance at the beginning of January, if that is satisfactory. Don't spend it all at once, and far be it from me to tell you what should be done with your money, but I feel that a certain Mr Lewis should perhaps be rewarded in some way for discovering the true worth of these artefacts.

I'm sure you have already considered this, and please forgive me for mentioning it!

Thank you once again. I haven't been so excited since I was allowed to touch the Bard's willy ours sincerely, Professor Adrian Bytheway.

The rather unfortunate spacing error at the end did add a bizarre note, and was obviously typed in great haste by a very excited professor. Ruby just stood there, staring at the piece of paper that accompanied it. This was wealth beyond her wildest dreams. The family lived in a council house and Len's wages just about paid for the weekly bills, with precious little to splash out on holidays or clothes. Ruby had always been very careful, meticulously writing down every payment in a neat notebook, and nothing was wasted. This insignificant-looking little piece of paper with a scrawled signature had the power to completely transform their world. It was like winning the pools or the premium bonds. The only difference was, there would be another, identical one to follow! She stood, just holding the cheque for several minutes, in a daze, until she finally snapped out of her reverie and realized that she was still on the front doorstep, frozen to the spot. Her next-door neighbour, Frank, said hello.

"Security van, eh?" he smiled. "Len's wages?"

"No," replied Ruby. "It was the, erm, catalogue, come to deliver Auntie Deirdre's son Graham's corduroy trousers. At five pounds per pair, you can't be too careful!" She knew she was rambling, but in her defence, she had had rather a big shock.

* * *

It was a heavily Brycreemed, singed and generally Hitler-like creature that fell out of Freddie Fielding's barbershop that Friday evening. The last time he had emerged from that house of horrors, it was into dense fog, and part of David was hoping for the same this evening, to hide his severe new haircut. He had always hated the back of his head, because he perceived it as bulging and skull-like. He most admired heads like the one that actor James Garner had, which was modelled loosely on a shoebox. Unfortunately, after Freddie had done his work, this bulge effect was all the more prominent. At least he would have the weekend to wash the hair and try to reshape it a little, prior to running the gauntlet at school on Monday. To ease the pain, he was given his Cadbury's penny chocolate and crossed over the road, whence he proceeded in the direction of his grandparent's house. He had not been past Miss Kettle's shop since the funeral, but he had heard that it was shortly to be taken over by new people, if it hadn't been already. He hoped that they were a tad more child-friendly than their predecessor had been. That said, she did leave him an enormous amount of money; a tiny proportion of which he was about to give back, in exchange for a Sopwith Camel.

As he approached the shop, he was pleased to see that the lights were on. He pushed open the front door, which activated the bell, and stood, waiting to be served. When no one came after a few minutes, he rang the brass bell on the counter. Still no one arrived. The expression *déjà vu* has been used once before to describe David's feelings. Now he was feeling a sense of *déjà vu* squared to the power of three, with knobs on. Cautiously, he took the well-trodden path, through the gap in the counter, and called into the back room. No answer. With a huge lump in his throat, he turned his gaze to the right and down. Miss Kettle lay flat out on the ground, with a huge bump on her brow.

"Bloody hell!" she moaned, rubbing her battered bonce, and trying unsuccessfully to haul herself up from the floor. David, ever the Boy Scout, dashed to help her.

"If I've done that once since I've been here, I've done it a thousand times," she said, with as big a smile as she could muster. "It's that bloomin' big old till. You leave it open and bend down to retrieve a coin, and then it has yer!"

She stood at the counter, supporting herself with one hand, and rubbing the old bean with the other.

"Hang on!" she said, groggily. "I recognize you! You're little David Day aren't you?"

David, who was bought up by his parents never to lie, admitted that he was. Miss Kettle's sister, strangely enough also called Miss Kettle, said she was pleased to meet him. She knew Ruby and Len from Tenbury, and she was aware how he'd helped her late sister in various ways. Formalities over, she asked how she could help *him*. He told her that he'd tried several times to buy a Sopwith Camel, and each time he'd been met with a shop keeper whose reluctance to help him could be put down entirely to unconsciousness or death, rather than malice. Oh, and there was the time in Tenbury when he'd just been too stunned to speak.

Miss Kettle stepped over to the window, and picked up the aeroplane kit.

"I trust this is what you've been after?" she said, smiling broadly. David couldn't equate smiles with Miss Kettle. It just didn't seem right. She'd have to dye her hair blonde or something, so he didn't keep thinking she was the other one. He thanked her brokenly and handed over the funds.

"That won't be necessary," she insisted. "In fact, it won't ever be necessary, young man. Whenever you see a toy you like, pop in, and it's yours, for nothing, on me!"

David said that he couldn't possibly, and so on and so forth, but she wouldn't hear of it.

"You will report here, at least once a week, and choose something. Don't go mad, of course, or I'll be broke. I'm only looking after it for a short while anyway, so it won't kill me. My nephew is taking the shop over. He's a nice man. I'll tell him to look after you. Oh yes, and I'll warn him about the till too. I'd hate for you to discover him on his back. You've had more than enough of that, I reckon!"

David laughed.

"So, young man. It's a deal. If you don't choose a toy once a week, I'll come round to box your ears. Understand? My sister was a bit of an old crone. I know that. She'd had a pretty tough life, what with one thing and another. Just before her heart attack, she changed her will to include you, so you must have been special to her, in her own funny way. And now, my lad, you can be special to me too. I'll see you, on the dot, next week. I'll keep a Spitfire for you, if you haven't already got one!"

She shook his hand, and he left the shop a very happy boy indeed. Things had been going badly, and now, at last, things were starting to go the right way. People were chucking money at him, and this, he felt was to be encouraged.

CHAPTER 24

The Play's the Thing

All over Brierley Bank, well-scrubbed children with neatly knotted ties were coming out of their houses, accompanied by parents dressed in their Sunday best. Factory workers who would never normally put a tie around their necks had done so this evening, though some of the older ones were unsure as to whether it was *de rigueur* to have them under or over their pullovers. Those children who weren't in school uniform had large raincoats on, to disguise the biblical clothing beneath.

The trickle of people soon became a flood, as the good folk of the town joined ranks to forge onwards to the lovely little school at the centre of their community. The prefects were in position on the doors to offer programmes (cover design by David Day. Class 6L) and show the various dignitaries to their reserved seats. The mayor and his wife, in matching gold chains, spoke to the vicar in the foyer, while their chauffeur leant against the Daimler outside, puffing on a crafty Senior Service. Mr Bingham, the P.E. teacher, was shepherding huge tribes of shepherds backstage, while Mrs Hancox assembled her ensemble on the chairs in front of the stage and made sure they all had their music.

187

Meanwhile, Mr Lewis was busy arranging the choir in neat rows. The recorder group unpacked their instruments from their regulation mustard-coloured corduroy bags, and busied themselves by cleaning the foul-smelling spit and debris out of them. Mrs Hancox sat herself down at the piano and leaned across to talk to them all, telling them to do their best and not be too nervous. The need to involve most of the children had caused Mr Evans, the drama teacher, to veer from the original story a little, and the hillsides were soon to be seriously overpopulated with shepherds, angels, townsfolk and innkeepers. Those who weren't on stage were doing readings at the lectern, operating the lights and curtains or moving props between scenes. In short, Brierley Bank's Bethlehem was only slightly less busy than the Bedlam that was Birmingham on a Saturday night. The key players, Joseph and Mary, were locked in their trailers and refusing to sign autographs. At least three of the supporting cast had been copiously sick with nerves, but the star of the show, the baby Jesus, was unmoved by the goings on around him, ever the seasoned professional. When you're a doll wrapped in two tea towels, lent with the kind permission of Gillian Homer, 3C, stage fright isn't an issue.

Meanwhile, Mr Perriman sat in his office, sadly reflecting on his troubles and dreading the bittersweet evening ahead. He loved his children and they loved him, even when he'd had to whack the occasional backside with his dreaded cane. They may not have loved him right there and then, or even for the next day or so, but they soon forgave and forgot, and in the future would probably inform anyone who would listen that it did them no harm whatsoever.

Sam Perriman was not looking forward to what he had to do. He would have to sit through this lovely show, full of cute little kids in tea towels shouting out their lines, no doubt with tears welling in his eyes, and then come onstage to thank everyone for their efforts. He'd tell all the parents that they should be proud of their children, and thank Mrs Hancox for organizing the choir and the recorder ensemble. Then he'd tell them all that his beloved school was closing for good at the end of summer term, and that he was retiring.

It was six-thirty, and the early birds were arriving. The hall was buzzing now, with teachers and school children taking up their positions. At seven, he would have to put on a brave face and greet everyone, but for now, he preferred to be alone.

Mr Perriman was a churchgoing Christian gentleman, and a teetotaller. He had never even tried alcohol, because his parents before him were of like mind, and he never drank anything stronger than PG Tips. He envied those who, before some nerve-wracking public speaking engagement, could take a quick snort of whisky or a poison of their choosing, and suddenly become confident and even devil-may-care. Normally he didn't get nervous. Anyone who has addressed children and parents from a lofty stage for forty years should be well past worrying about that kind of thing. Tonight, however, was a different story. Tonight, he had to break a good many hearts, his own included. He walked over to his cabinet, where he kept his trophies, some very old school logbooks and his Victorian bible. There was a lovely Stuart Crystal decanter with six glasses, which the PTA had bought him for his sixtieth. He hadn't the heart to tell them it wouldn't be used. There was also a bottle of scotch, which a well-meaning parent had got him, so that his decanter could be christened. It too was untouched.

Then, for some inexplicable reason, he opened the cabinet, and took out the bottle. He uncorked it and sniffed the contents. A shudder went through his entire body. The smell was just awful. It was alien to all he held dear. He poured a tiny drop into one of the cut glass tumblers, and sipped it. The taste, as he suspected, was as evil as the smell. He carried the bottle and glass over to his desk, and tried it again. Everyone he knew drank alcohol, and yet it tasted dreadful. Perhaps his taste buds were not the same as other men's. How anyone could even compare this septic liquid to PG Tips was beyond him. It was going to be flushed down the nearest toilet. He hated himself for being tempted in his hour of need, and a feeling of self-pity and self-loathing crept over him.

Hadn't Jesus ever been tempted?

Yes, of course. He was, after all, only human. Mr Perriman tried once more to tolerate this ghastly concoction, prior to flushing it away. Perhaps just a medicinal glassful would vanquish his nerves. He held his nose and swigged the glass down in one. His cheeks were now flushed red, for he was a man with absolutely no tolerance to alcohol. The taste, he was forced to admit, was *marginally* more pleasant that time. This stuff, vile though it undoubtedly was, did slightly improve, the more one drank it. He poured another tumblerful, and then promised himself that that would be sufficient for the task ahead. He dutifully swallowed it, whereupon a mighty thirst came upon him - one of biblical proportions. He decided it would be wise to visit the lavatory prior to greeting his guests - one didn't want to be seen leaving halfway through a performance; it would seem like bad manners. He rose unsteadily to his feet and tried to walk towards the door. He had his own lavatory adjacent to his office, so he didn't have to stagger far. His gait, once so sure-footed, was now two steps forward followed by one sideways. He backtracked to scoop up the bottle and glass, which he thought he might need for the journey.

His study, which he could usually depend upon to keep still, was wobbling all over the place, and, for some reason, this made him laugh. Mr Perriman, unlike Ruby, was not one of life's gigglers, but something had stirred him, and he was finding it difficult to stop.

Getting into the lavatory proved difficult too, as there appeared to be two locks on the door. He eventually located the more solid of the two, and fell heavily, fully-clothed, onto the seat, spilling around half of the bottle's contents on the linoleum. This amused the dishevelled head teacher, who sat for several minutes, staring at the spillage and smiling. The expensive cut-glass tumbler slipped from his grasp and joined the spilt whisky on the floor, but thankfully, the Stuart Crystal was made of stern stuff, and miraculously refused to break. This too was a great source of amusement to Mr Perriman. He celebrated his good fortune with a large swig from the bottle, followed closely by several more, whereupon he became quickly maudlin, and fell into a deep sleep.

Back in the hall, things were hotting up nicely, and the room was full to capacity. The seats had long since been filled, and it was standing room only at the back. Arguments began to break out as families tried to reserve seats for latecomers, but the punctual ones were having none of this, and tempers were fraying. The arrival of the vicar, who was endeavouring to pour oil over troubled waters, stopped all disagreements dead when he tactfully reminded the ashamed trouble-makers who the real star of the show was, and what he stood for.

David and his parents had arrived early, because he played the clarinet in the band. They grabbed the best seats they could, and he went off to join his fellow musicians. Mally, who couldn't play a note, but knew about animals, was a natural choice for shepherd No. 2. Meanwhile, Mr Lewis was pumping beads of sweat from his brow and wondering where on earth his boss had got to. He'd quickly popped down to the Head's office and knocked the door, but there was no reply. This wasn't like Mr Perriman. He was usually punctuality personified. There was nothing else Mr Lewis could do but take over, at least until he returned.

It was seven o'clock now, and everyone was in place. The heavy purple velvet stage curtain was now closed, and the children in the band began to place their music sheets on their stands, ready for the first piece. A gaggle - if that is the correct collective pronoun - of shepherds, and a trio of wise men stood rooted to their markers, waiting for 'overture and beginners'. The parents were all chatting and pointing out their offspring to myopic elderly grandparents, and Mr Lewis, looking flustered as hell, strode up onto the stage.

"Lord Mayor, Lady Mayoress, vicar, ladies and gentlemen, children, good evening and a very warm welcome to Brierley Bank Junior School. Unfortunately, Mr Perriman appears to have, erm, been called away on an urgent matter, so I'm master of ceremonies until he returns. We have a lovely Nativity play for you tonight, folks, so I'll shut up and let the show commence."

He shot off stage sharpish, mopping the sweat from his brow just like Louis Armstrong always did when he sang 'Wonderful World'. The house lights dimmed and Mrs Hancox played a few bars of something or other on the piano, which must have been a secret signal, because a load of freshly-scrubbed choir boys and girls stood up suddenly and began singing a pretty tune about Bethlehem. This ended in due course, and it went down big with the assembled multitude, which applauded with gusto. Two studious-looking and immaculately turned out upper-school children, one of each gender, then walked up to the lectern directly in front of the velvet curtain and to the right-hand side. They took it in turns to deliver their lines, which could best be described as loud, workman-like, but perhaps lacking in feeling or variation of tone. A sterling joint effort, nonetheless, and invaluable for setting the scene. As they spoke, the velvet curtains parted with the tell-tale jerkiness that suggested two ropes were being heaved on by two underpowered stage-hands, and a marvellous tableau was eventually revealed. This was greeted with 'oohs' and 'aahs' by the large contingent within the crowd who were obviously avid followers of 'Take your Pick', the game show with the fabulous prizes.

A bank, made of the same plastic grass that greengrocers use to deck their windows, filled the back half of the stage. In front of this was a little street scene, with assorted biblical types going about their business, scrubbing floors vigorously, selling fruit, and chatting animatedly. The whole scene was backed by a lovely night sky full of stars, which were painted onto a giant panel. A hole had been cut out of the panel to accommodate a hundred watt light bulb, so that the important star would shine brighter than the rest.

Joseph, who seemed rather young and puny to have such a manly beard, was walking alongside Mary, who was twice as tall, and heavily pregnant with pillow. She sat side-saddle on a stuffed grey wooden horse with wheels, which was being pulled along by Joseph with a short rein. The choir stood and gave a stirring version of 'Little Donkey', which brought the house down. Then the two travellers paused at the Inn, where Mary dismounted.

Two new speakers, smaller and even more *staccato* than the last, kept the audience abreast of the latest developments. It appeared that the Inn was seriously oversubscribed, and due to fire regulations, or the fact that Joseph wasn't wearing a tie, the bouncer had refused entry. At this point, the choir stood up again, and after a few bars from Mrs Hancox, they slogged away at a soulful little number in a variety of simultaneous key signatures, which laid it on thickly about the plight of the homeless.

Job done, the choir took to their seats once more, and the sorry couple and their 'Dunlopillo' offspring staggered off in the direction of the stable block. After another pair of orators had done their worst, Joseph asked if there was any room at the stables, and a rough, rustic type begrudgingly allowed them in to doss down amongst the straw. So far so good, one might say, and all exactly according to plan, if we are to believe the good book.

The velvet curtains jerked shut again, and Mrs Hancox struck up a cheerful intro at the piano. This was the cue for David to play a brief clarinet solo, prior to the whole band joining in. His front milk-tooth, which had irritatingly been coming loose for some time, chose this inconvenient moment to separate from his gums and wedge itself firmly in the reed of his instrument, causing a violent squealing noise instead of the Acker Bilk-like vibrato he had hoped for. There followed an embarrassing silence, due to the fact that the clarinet was now completely incapacitated, and David's hot little face became almost camouflaged against the rich colour of the purple velvet. Thinking on her feet, Mrs Hancox repeated the intro and played his part on piano, so that the band knew where to come in. Meanwhile, David suddenly became acutely interested in studying his sheet music, and pretended the audience weren't there.

It was Len's custom to temporarily stop breathing whenever David performed, and though naturally disappointed that his son's performance had come to an abrupt end, he was nevertheless grateful that his lungs had not been taxed on this occasion. Other than this, the musical interlude - mere subterfuge while the scenery was shifted - went well. The curtains opened once more, and this time there was a hillside made of plastic grass, with three tea-towelled shepherds and three plywood sheep to match. The customary pair of narrators did their bit, and left via the stage steps.

The diminutive, heavily-bearded shepherds were chatting of this and that, when suddenly there was a big theatrical flash of light and smoke, which caused several of the older members of the audience to shriek with fright. Then, out of the smoke, came an angel with a wand, suspended against the night sky by a one-inch thick rope which was painted dark blue as an attempt at camouflage. She was spinning around uncontrollably for several seconds before a long matt black rod appeared stage-left and poked her a little, to enable her to face the front, where she mercifully stayed.

The vision had obviously stirred the simple peasant folk - the ones on stage, not the audience - because they all fell dramatically to their knees in awe, and covered their faces. David Nixon, who shared a name with the famous television magician, was a rather heavy-handed boy, and he threw himself into the role rather too forcefully, hitting the deck like a sack of potatoes. Immediately, all three plywood sheep fell over with the impact, and became invisible to the

195

stunned audience. One wag near the back shouted loudly: "Bloody hell, David Nixon's made the sheep disappear!" and was immediately shushed by several disgusted grandmas.

The sudden demise of David's sheep came as a shock to the assembled shepherds, as it did to David. From the orchestra pit, he saw the three sheep that had taken him six months and around seventy-six jigsaw blades to create retire from public life after about fifteen seconds. Fifteen minutes, as later prescribed by Andy Warhol, he could have accepted, but fifteen seconds was just too cruel to bear. After all, the next time they were dusted off for action, he'd be at a different school. He didn't have time to dwell on this disaster for too long, however, because he had to remove the tooth and broken reed, and replace the latter with a new one in time for the band piece, entitled 'While shepherds watched their flocks by night.'

As the band struck up the opening salvo, the untrained musical ear could have been mistaken for thinking it had come, by mistake, to a Schoenberg concert performed in a small shed full of noisy pigs, cockerels and donkeys that were simultaneously being injected with blunt needles. A lengthy analogy, but no other would have fully expressed the sounds escaping from the orchestra pit. That said, the traditional Nativity play is never intended to be about accuracy of note, quality of tone, or even consistent key signatures. It is about the love of parents for their offspring, which hopefully transcends all.

Next up was a rather podgy girl with plaited hair and freckles that suggested she had been sunbathing for extended periods with a colander on her face. To say that she couldn't sing would have been churlish and unfair.

Perhaps the best way of putting it was that she sang in a way that gave no one (except maybe her immediate family) any pleasure. Her rendition of the misleadingly titled 'Silent Night' was at least short and to the point. Even television's talent scout and presenter, Hughie Green, who could stomach most things as long as they emanated from the mouths of cute children or plucky octogenarians, would have struggled.

The curtain closed on the tableau once more, and while scenery was being rearranged, assorted singers and recorder groups did their best to mask the din backstage. Two more narrators arrived at the lectern, and one of them was about halfway into her *spiel*, when the other suddenly screamed loudly. He whispered something to his fellow speaker, who then also began screaming hysterically and flailing her arms around. Perplexed, Mr Lewis dashed up the steps and appeared to be examining the girl closely. The audience could make nothing of this strange behaviour whatsoever.

Finally, after much agitation on all sides, Mr Lewis removed two huge locusts from the hapless child's coiffure. When the commotion had died down and the girl had been taken away for intense counselling, the curtains opened for the final time to reveal the stable, with wise men in cardboard crowns, shepherds, townsfolk, stuffed donkey *et al*. David was particularly pleased to see his sheep had made it down from yon distant hills for the finale, thanks entirely to the quick thinking of the kindly Mr Lewis. Interestingly, David Nixon, the head shepherd, had now been strategically placed at the other end of the stage.

A small boy who looked too young for the job now strode to the lectern, squared and rearranged his papers, newsreader-style, and told the audience all about the wise men, who came, apparently, from afar. In spite of his diminutive stature, he had a confident voice, and didn't seem to need the scripts, once in full flow. In fact, he did extremely well, until he announced that the baby Jesus was to be given 'Gold, Frankenstein and Mirth'.

A ripple of laughter travelled around the audience. This seemed to displease the boy, who until then had been by far the best of the speakers, and he stamped his foot angrily and screamed "Shut up! Shut up!" before stomping off in a huff, into the arms of Mrs Hancox. The main actors in the tableau, Joseph, Mary, the shepherds and the wise men, were getting to their speaking parts now, and going at an incredible lick. Mary was holding the baby Jesus in her arms and accepting gifts from all and sundry, when all of a sudden a miracle happened. Little Jesus, who had been silent until that point, suddenly spoke. He said:

"My nappy's wet mommy. I love you mommy!"

The cast just looked on in wonderment, and so did the audience. Mary stood up in disgust, the front of her costume soaked through with holy water.

"It's peed all over me!" she squealed.

The audience members had acted with remarkable restraint during the initial vanishing sheep miracle, but this second incident caused the floodgates to open, and a tidal wave of uncontrollable hysterics swept through the hall, with Ruby Day surfing on top of it. Mrs Homer in the second row whispered red-faced to her husband, "They've only gone and used our Gillian's doll for Jesus; the one that talks and wets itself! We'll never live it down!"

Thankfully, Mally had the presence of mind to grind on, albeit through tears of laughter, by loudly shouting out his lines and pulling everyone together. A few more speakers and a quick carol wrapped up the show, and to rapturous applause and cheering, the curtain jerked across for the last time. Mr Lewis bounded on stage, and appealed for silence. If the crowd had got their way, they'd have clapped and cheered till the baby Jesus gave them an encore, or second coming, as it is often called, but this was not a pop concert, and the children didn't have anything else up their sleeves.

"Thank you folks!" he said, grinning like a Cheshire cat. "Well, I'm sure you'll agree that we've just witnessed a very eventful few days in Bethlehem! Give your children one more round of applause. You'll remember this performance for a good many years, I'm sure!"

His facial expression suddenly turned from jovial to grave, as he remembered his next task. He appealed for order, and eventually it came.

"Lord Mayor, Lady Mayoress, vicar, ladies and gentlemen, children. If I could have your attention for a few minutes, I now have some serious and rather upsetting news for you all. Mr Perriman should have been here tonight to tell you about this, but as you can see, he has not been able to make it. Such is the seriousness of the situation; he has been forced to miss the Nativity play, something he wouldn't do for the world, under normal circumstances. I can only presume he is, at this moment, in some small meeting room or other, trying to resolve matters. You see, we had a letter recently from the council, about the state of the school buildings. As you are probably already aware, the science block has been condemned, due to subsidence. Also, the roofs and window frames throughout the premises are in desperate need of replacing. The council have thought long and hard about this, and have reached the conclusion that they cannot meet the cost of repairs. They wish to close this lovely old school, and amalgamate us with the new, considerably larger Thornwood School, a mile away."

The audience had been deadly silent throughout this speech, and now they were leaning over and whispering to each other. Several voices shouted their opposition, and a few seemed to be levelling their anger at the mayor, who was looking distinctly uncomfortable. Mr Lewis continued.

"Ladies and Gentlemen, please! No one is more upset than I over this, but we can't solve anything by getting angry. I am totally opposed to this move myself, and Mr Perriman is beside himself with worry, but I can see what the council people mean. It has been estimated at many thousands of pounds to fill the subsidence with concrete and replace all those windows, not to mention the roofing. Their argument is that there is a huge school up the road, with not enough pupils in it. I can see their point."

"It's a bloody horrible, soulless modern place!" shouted an angry parent. "What we have here is just perfect. Can't we club together? Hold raffles, sponsored events?"

Mr Lewis shook his head.

"It's impossible. It's just too great a sum I'm afraid. We'll be sending you all a letter this week, of course, but I feel that the end has come for this building. As to the fate of us teachers, that is still undecided. Some may have to go, as duplication with the Thornwood staff could be a problem. Hopefully, this will be minimal."

He glanced down at the choir, and noticed that several children were now crying. Biting his lip, he tried to sum up.

"Anyway folks, if this does have to happen, it won't be till the end of summer term next year, and remember, it's not over till it's over, as they say. If I know our Head, he'll be fighting the good fight as we speak. Never say die, Dai, he said to me earlier today. It's nearly Christmas time, a time of miracles, after all!"

The assembled multitude didn't hold much hope of miracles, judging by their faces. Gradually, they began to stand and make their way to the exits. Mr Lewis came down from the stage and shook a few hands. David had left the band, and was heading for his parents. Several minutes later, the three of them arrived at the exit, where Mr Lewis was still saying goodbye to distraught parents.

"Can I see you for a second?" asked Len. Mr Lewis made his excuses, and they slipped behind the curtains onto the stage.

"We just wanted to give you a bit of money, you know, for helping us with the Shakespeare stuff. Without you, the box and its contents would probably have been 'improved' by our David, and then left outside in the rain by accident."

David gave them a look, and he meant it to sting.

"Thanks folks, but it's not necessary," Mr Lewis assured them. "Really. I'm just happy for you. The thrill for me was seeing the stuff; being a part of history, if only for a day or two. *There's* something to tell the grandkids, eh?"

This was but stage one in the ritual negotiations that human beings subject each other to. He was a good man, but secretly he wouldn't have minded a hundred quid for his efforts. He knew what traditionally came next – The Black Country Stand-Off. Len would say, "I insist!" Mr Lewis would say, "No no, I couldn't possibly!", whereupon Len would tell him that he would be mortally wounded unless he accepted. Mr Lewis would then 'reluctantly' take the cheque, and everyone was happy. It was ever thus, but never more so than in the Black Country.

Len reached into his jacket pocket and produced a chequebook. He unclipped a Parker pen from his breast pocket and began to write, using David's back as a desk. Mr Lewis protested too much - just like the travelling player in Hamlet that Queen Gertrude complained about - and kept mumbling about it not being necessary, and how he was embarrassed. Len passed the cheque to David, who presented it to his teacher. Mr Lewis took it and thanked them profusely. He was about to slip it into his coat unread, as is traditional, but Ruby coughed, and respectfully asked him to check if the sum was satisfactory. Assuring her that any amount would suffice, he reached for his reading glasses and reluctantly studied the wording. Len's writing was never the clearest, but the words and figures were perfectly legible.

'Pay Mr D. Lewis, the sum of one hundred thousand pounds.'

"Erm, Mr Day, you've put the noughts in the wrong place!" he spluttered.

"I'm a tool-maker," replied Len. "I know about numbers, and especially the 'thou'. They're in the right place, my friend!"

Mr Lewis grasped a nearby plywood sheep for support.

"Repair the school, and keep the change, Mr Lewis. It's an incentive for you to get keen quotes. If you *still* feel guilty, send a few quid to the woman from Henley!"

CHAPTER 25

Much Ado about Nothing

Mr Perriman sat at his desk, looking dishevelled. He woke up at five-thirty with one hell of a stiff neck and a headache, the pain of which only Miss Kettle could fully understand. His mouth felt as though a plague rat had crawled into it while he slept, died and slowly decomposed, and his double-chin was stubbly with grey hairs. He was desperate for water, even though he'd already swigged down at least three tumblerfuls of the stuff. Luckily, his wife was visiting relatives in Inverness, or search parties would have been summoned long since, and then he'd have been for it. His brief dalliance with the demon drink was, thankfully, over. If that was how it made you feel the day after, they could bloody well keep it, was his reckoning.

It was a head teacher lacking his usual 'get up and go' that groaned "Come in!" when someone without rapped his door rather too vigorously. In strode a rather more refreshed and bullish-looking Mr Lewis, who bade the sorry remains a cheery good morning.

"Goodness me!" exclaimed the Welshman, as he examined his dishevelled boss. "What on earth happened to you?"

Mr Perriman, not a man who enjoyed telling lies, nevertheless did.

"Oh, I had a violent tummy bug. Terrible! Had to dash to the loo at seven last night, just before I was due to greet the parents and so on. Coming out of both ends with a vengeance, it was. I was so ill that I couldn't make it to the door to even warn you, I'm afraid!"

"Dear me! I am sorry. Okay now?"

"Bit rough, but I've stopped being sick." Even when he lied, this Head teacher needed a basis of truth to help him along. "Ask Gwen from the canteen to do me a bit of breakfast old son, there's a pal."

"Of course," said Mr Lewis.

"How did it go last night?" asked Mr Perriman. "Did you broach the dreaded subject, or will I have to let them all know via the post? I really didn't want to saddle you with that. I understand if you chose to defer."

"No, I told them, and it didn't go down well, I can tell you."

Mr Lewis reached for his envelope as he spoke. "Do you believe in Father Christmas, Sam?"

Mr Perriman looked at him askance. It crossed his mind that his deputy may have been drinking, but he was hardly in a position to criticize.

"You know?" continued Mr Lewis, "Santa Claus - big bloke with a beard; comes around at Christmas, delivering presents!"

"Yes," snapped Mr Perriman, a mite tetchily, for this self-inflicted headache had made him bad tempered. "I know who it is. No, I stopped believing in all that a long time ago."

"Well, you should be ashamed. Start believing again, as I do."

Mr Lewis handed him the envelope. Mr Perriman opened it, and looked at the contents. It was the cheque.

"Now do you believe in Santa Claus?" he smiled.

* * *

Over the next few days, Messers Perriman and Lewis saw various council officials and eventually hammered out a deal. It was agreed in principle to keep the school open, as long as the school could finance the repairs themselves. Mr Lewis asked his fellow teachers to deputize while he spent whole days ringing around for competitive quotes from reputable tradesmen. Once the quotes were agreed, the work was scheduled to commence just after the Christmas break, with difficult repairs to be carried out on weekends, so as not to disrupt the pupils.

As the two men took a breather and sipped at their coffees after a hard morning's negotiating, Mr Lewis spoke.

"You know, Head, our young David is a one-off, don't you agree? He rounded up the entire school and dragged them to the funeral of a woman most of them couldn't stick at any price. He's paid for all the children to have a party this Christmas. Now he's donated the incredible sum of a hundred thousand pounds to save the school! Okay, he cost us nearly that much in jigsaw blades this term, but it's still bloody remarkable."

The Head smiled benignly and nodded.

"I'm thinking we ought to commemorate him in some way. It's the least we can do, don't you think?"

The Head agreed wholeheartedly. "Let me ponder that," he said, "but right now, I've got a letter to write, and for once, it'll be a joy to compose!"

A few days later, the parents were told of the school's reprieve, and there was a communal sigh of relief that could be heard as far away as Wolverhampton.

CHAPTER 26

Jelly and Ice Cream

The Day family still could not fully comprehend the meaning of their windfall. Ruby and Len talked about the best way of investing it, and agreed that David should have a sizeable amount stashed away in his building society for when he was older. They did likewise. They also agreed that they were happy at the house they lived in, though they could easily afford bigger and better. With that came new neighbours and new problems, which neither wanted. Len was less fond of his job, however. He'd been a tool-maker for too many years, and whilst he loved the company of his fellow workers, the dirty, heavy work was grinding him down. What he really loved was pottering around in his tool shed, and especially making old-fashioned wooden toys, which he sold to friends and relatives, usually for just a touch less than the cost of the raw materials. He was astute in that way.

After much soul-searching, he decided to hand in his notice and turn his hobby into a small business. He didn't have to earn a lot, just as long as he didn't lose any. He would sell his wares to the local toy shops, and, encouragingly, Miss Kettle had already agreed to take whatever he could produce.

The Day family did splash out on one expensive item, however. Len came back one afternoon with a glossy caravan brochure, and a week or so later a brand new, eight-berth luxury caravan was being sited in Tenbury, where their old one used to stand. It had a proper lavatory too, which saved them having to dice with death by using the odious 'Chemi-Khasi' or suffer those awful midnight dashes to the breezeblock lavvies, clad only in slippers and dressing gowns. The fact that the second cheque had not yet arrived didn't worry anyone unduly. It was guaranteed in January, and the British Museum was hardly a fly-by-night outfit. One look at their letter and caravan salesmen were bending over backwards to part with their goods with a promise of payment within the month.

David continued spreading *largesse*, and bought Mally a beautiful split-cane fishing rod with all the accessories as a Christmas present. It was hidden under David's bed, already gift- wrapped, so that Mally didn't find it before the big day. David would have to invent some unlikely story as to how he'd managed to afford it, as the Shakespeare windfall was still a closely-guarded secret. Then there was the problem of Mally's guilt to consider, when he couldn't reciprocate. This newly-acquired wealth was causing more problems than David had imagined. One didn't wish to appear flash, after all.

Meanwhile, schooldays seemed an anticlimax after the excitement of the Nativity play. The older children were summoned to help tidy up and pack the plastic grass, props and costumes into boxes. The plywood sheep were being stored in the area beneath the stage until the following year, and David and Mally were trying to herd them towards the door when young Tubbs appeared.

"Hello you two," he squawked. "I've got a puzzle for you. A man's peacock lays an egg in the next-door neighbour's garden. Who does the egg belong to?"

"Peacocks are male. They don't lay eggs," yawned Mally, who knew his birds.

"Oh!" said Tubby, deflated. "Okay then. There's a frog dead in the middle of a pond, and…"

"We've heard it!" said David. "If you *will* insist on telling jokes, tell us funny ones. For example, there were two flies on some dog poo, and one of them did a trump, and the other one said, 'Do you mind? I'm eating my breakfast!'"

Tubbs was not abreast. He had the baffled look of a young man awaiting a punch line. David gave him a scornful look and reverted to his shepherding duties in disgust.

"Tell you what, Tubbsy," said Mally, in conciliatory mode. "Promise you won't tell us any more useless jokes or ask us any more of your rubbish riddles and we'll let you help us put the sheep away. Then - if you'll agree in writing to stop boring us to death with all that nonsense, and sign it - you can fetch the ball when me and Dave play cricket this dinner time."

Tubbs was beside himself with glee, as any right-minded child would have been, having been chosen by two prefects to help store a few plywood sheep under a stage *and* to retrieve a cork ball from the boundaries of a freezing cricket pitch in December. School life, he felt, was definitely on the up.

*

The hall was cleared and mopped ready for its next event, the Christmas party, which was being held on the Thursday afternoon before the final day of term. Thanks to the generosity of the Day family, there really was something to celebrate.

Trestle tables were laid out in rows, each dressed with red paper tablecloths. Balloons were inflated and paper cups delivered. Hundreds of jellies arrived in a choice of the four house colours, while jolly dinner ladies in crêpe paper party hats and pinafores laid crackers on tables. Parents were asked to supply knives, forks and spoons, which had to have coloured wool tied around the handles for ease of identification later on. This system had been used for many years, in spite of the fact that most parents used the same colours and owned the same make of cutlery, meaning that correct identification was nigh-on impossible come four o'clock.

There is a certain breed of woman in the Black Country and almost certainly elsewhere, for whom making cakes is nothing short of an obsession. Their families leave them to their own devices for the afternoon, and when they return home they are greeted by mounds of assorted cakes arranged on china plates. The cake-makers simply cannot help themselves – it is a form of addiction. Any school, in order to be successful, must know how to harness the power of these mysterious creatures and give them a purpose. Through a network of spies, they are sought out and offered a legitimate reason to bake a cake, and they jump at it. It gives them their *'raison d'etre'*.

Brierley Bank School, like all other schools, kept top secret lists of such women. When news got round of the party, armies of them came out of the woodwork, like the zombies that infest foggy smuggling villages down in Cornwall. At midday, they arrived, in ones and twos at first, carrying baking trays wrapped in greaseproof paper, joining forces until they became a battalion. Into the hall they came, with their butterfly cakes, kitten cakes bedecked with Smarties, and exotic concoctions sprinkled with 'hundreds and thousands'. Then they would return to their homes and vanish as mysteriously as they had appeared, and lie dormant until their next calling.

The dinner ladies, meanwhile, were now creating the European sandwich mountain, with cheese, Spam, corned beef and turkey. Crates of Tizer, dandelion and burdock and lemonade were offloaded from the pop-man's lorry. Teachers were on their hands and knees in the staff room, creating 'pin the tail on the donkey' and 'pass the parcel' games, and Mrs Hancox, in the absence of a radio, was seconded to provide incidental music at the piano. Mr Perriman even ordered hundreds of Ladybird books, so that each child would receive a present from Father Christmas in his grotto; a Father Christmas whose resemblance to Cedric from the café was nothing short of uncanny, as was his grasp of the local dialect.

Everything was ready. At precisely one o'clock, hundreds of over-excited children burst into the hall and stripped it of its contents, like a swarm of locusts. If anyone had looked closely, they may possibly have observed several *real* locusts mixing freely with their human counterparts. Many of the science lab insects had not been accounted for, and were merrily reproducing like rabbits in the many nooks and crannies that the school offered. It was more likely that they were keeping out of the way this particular afternoon, however, as the average locust likes a quiet life. The cacophony emanating from the hall was truly deafening, as hundreds of stir-crazy kids began to let off steam. The rowdier contingent had realized the potential of jelly, not only as a foodstuff, but also as ammunition, while others were content to just grind fairy cakes underfoot or remove the unwanted ingredients from sandwiches and flick them at each other. Their table manners were, to say the very least, not quite to Swiss finishing school standard, but this was the end of the term, the school was saved, Christmas was but a few days away, and everything was damned-near perfect.

A few frenzied hours later, they were piling out of the school gates, loaded to the gunwales with trophy balloons and prizes, bags full of smelly P.E. clothing, someone else's colour-coded cutlery, and the peculiar paintings and *papier maché* sculptures that they had produced over the last term. If the state of the hall was anything to go by, they had certainly enjoyed David's secret benevolence. The staff members were sitting in a corner of the hall with the dinner ladies, dazed and confused, with shaking hands clutching plastic cups of strong tea and their crêpe paper party hats cocked at jaunty angles. Mr Lewis, his collar open and tie loosened, found just enough energy to open his mouth.

"Well, that was hard work. We could do with a real drink now, to celebrate, eh folks? Have you still got that nice bottle of whisky wasting away in your office, boss?"

Mr Perriman explained that, regrettably, he'd disposed of it earlier that month to a very good friend of his who actually enjoyed drinking the evil stuff. It was the best excuse he could think of at short notice. He munched an exhausted ham sandwich, whilst the locust making himself at home inside his crêpe paper hat had to make do with a small blob of raspberry jelly.

CHAPTER 27

A Winter's Tale

It was Christmas day - technically speaking, that is. Actually it was about six in the morning, and pitch black outside. David padded to the door of his parents' bedroom.

"Can I get up yet?" he asked, optimistically.

"The answer was no an hour ago. It was no half an hour ago, and, come to think of it, a quarter of an hour ago!" grunted his dishevelled and stubbly father. "Why should it be any different now?"

"It's been Christmas day for AGES!" argued David. "Can we get up please?"

Both parents knew that when David had a bee in his bonnet it was useless to resist, so Len crawled from his pit and went downstairs to make tea. David went down with him, and yelled with delight at the huge pillowcase full of presents that awaited him. He particularly loved seeing the half-eaten carrot and the empty sherry glass, and luckily, he, like most children, had not subjected this ritual to close scrutiny. If Father Christmas had accepted hospitality at every port of call, he would be feeling considerably sicker than Mr Perriman had recently been feeling by the early hours of

Christmas day. David dragged the sack back upstairs and placed it at the bottom of his parents' bed. Ruby grunted something vaguely festive and rolled over again. Never the world's best riser, she seemed to be getting worse of late. Even Len's offer of tea was refused, because she said she couldn't face it. In fairness, it was still the middle of the night, but one would have thought she would have been used to it, being Reuben's daughter.

Acres of coloured wrapping paper cluttered the bedroom, as toys, models, comic annuals and painting sets were revealed, each to the customary burst of gratitude, with the ancient flintlock pistol receiving a particularly ecstatic response. There were far more presents than he had received on previous Christmases, and both Ruby and Len were hoping and praying that the next cheque from the British Museum wasn't signed by Sir Barnes Wallace. As David furiously tore away, his eye was taken by a present so small that he could easily have missed it amongst the debris. It measured no more than two and a half inches by an inch and was covered in a rich red paper with a gold ribbon. He paused, curious, and picked it up. Len and Ruby looked at each other with half smiles. David gave them one of his theatrical 'what on earth's this?' expressions, and carefully unwrapped the outer paper. Inside was an England's Glory matchbox. His face took on a puzzled look.

"What's going on?" he asked, as he prised open the box. Inside, lying on a bed of straw was a tiny plastic model of a baby.

"I don't get it!" he said, waiting for his explanation.

Ruby sat up in bed. "It's a special present. Have you ever heard the saying, the best things come in small packages?"

He said that he had.

"Well, you're going to have a brother or sister," smiled Len.

"All being well," added Ruby, ever the cautious one.

David screamed with joy, so much so that Ruby had to calm him down, fearful of waking the neighbours. Her son's young life had been nigh-on idyllic, with one exception, if one discounted the odious Brett Spittle, school bully. Other children had someone to come home to, to play with and to look after. David hated being an only child, and though he had no shortage of friends, it just wasn't the same. For a few, stunned, glorious moments, all the other presents paled into insignificance.

"When I saw that little baby, at first I thought it was something to do with the Nativity play," he admitted. "I thought it might be a trick baby from Miss Kettle's shop that would pee on me when I opened the box!"

"We just wanted you to have someone that you couldn't eventually lose under the gas fire or accidentally squash," added Len, wearily. It was a nice line, but his logic was weak. David was more than capable of losing a baby under a gas fire.

Later, over breakfast, when Len and Ruby had exchanged slightly more prosaic gifts, David began to get curious about the finer points of their bombshell revalation, such as arrival times. Len explained that it would be six months before the baby was born, and apologized for what was going to be a considerable age difference.

"It's not so bad. You won't be able to play football with a baby right away; you have to grow 'em a bit first. You'll have to be a little patient, as the doctor said to the dwarf.

When you're twenty-two, your brother or sister will be about eleven. It won't seem such a gap then."

"I know it grows in your tummy, mom," frowned David earnestly, "but how did it get in there? I don't get it!"

Ruby and Len were beginning to look more sheepish than a pair of David's plywood sheep, which wasn't that difficult.

"They just, erm, arrive, son, when they're ready," explained Len, flushing slightly. "You know, like the Virgin Mary in the Nativity. It was the same when your mom was born. You've heard of the Virgin Berth haven't you?"

David nodded, but understood nothing. In fairness, he may well have got the joke had he seen it written down.

"Well, it's the same kind of thing," continued Len, eager to change the subject. "Look, it doesn't really matter how it got there. The important thing is, it's there – Doctor Rodgerson said so. That's why mom hasn't been feeling too well lately. Having babies can make you feel a bit queasy. Anyway, what shall we call it?"

"How about Bertha, if it's a girl, after my mother?" suggested Ruby. "Then she could be Berth Day!"

"Or what about Holly?" suggested Len. "And then she'd be Holly Day!"

"Very amusing," replied David. "What if it's a boy?"

"How about Knighton?" asked Len. "Knighton, the village where our caravan is, near Tenbury Wells, that is. We could start a new trend, naming babies after the place where they were conceived!"

"What's conceived mean?" said David.

"Never you mind!" said Ruby, giving Len one of her looks.

216

"Hang on a minute!" said David, groaning. "Knighton Day? You have to be kidding."

CHAPTER 28

All's Well That Ends Well

April 19th 2004

A big burgundy-coloured Mercedes convertible pulled up outside Brierley Bank Junior School, piloted by a slim fifty-year-old man with receding brown hair and wearing Ray-Bans. He pushed a button on the dashboard and the electric hood glided over from its storage compartment behind the rear seats to meet the front windscreen with a beautifully engineered Germanic clunk. Inside, David Day removed his sunglasses, substituting them for a pair of reading glasses in his breast pocket. He took an old black and white photograph from his wallet and stared at it.

The picture showed a young stick insect of a boy with a Hitler hairstyle sitting on the front steps of a council house, next to a slightly chubbier young lad with huge ears. The stick insect wore a long-sleeved jumper that his mother had knitted, shorts, and grey patterned socks, which looked suspiciously as though they'd been hoisted to the same height for the first time ever, just for the photograph. The other boy wore a white nylon shirt with a dishevelled tie. His arms, which were resting on his knees, looked thicker than the other boy's legs. His hairstyle, a mirror image of his friend's, had all the hallmarks of a Freddie Fielding special. Behind them was the front door and window of a small council house.

David stared at the photograph for what must have been fifteen minutes, without once looking away. He was completely mesmerised. The boy in the picture just wasn't *him* anymore. This child was someone quite separate to the fifty-year-old man he now was. David suddenly experienced a sickening feeling in the depths of his stomach. It was as though the child was someone he had once loved and lost, rather than just an earlier version of himself. The old photograph seemed to be acting as a kind of catalyst, jogging his dormant memory into recalling long-forgotten sights, sounds and smells with amazing clarity. He'd been used to going forward all of his life and never having a second to look back, but turning fifty had been a huge shock. Now he was taking stock of his life; realizing that he wasn't going to be around forever, and for some reason, he yearned to be reconnected with his childhood.

He'd tried and tried to make this connection, but his memory had been sketchy, until the day that his mother had given him the old photographs. It was one of these that he was entranced by now. It felt as though he'd dissolved into the scene, like 'Alice through the Looking Glass', and escaped into his golden, happy past, blissfully unaware of death, mortgages, stress and responsibility. At last he was remembering the detail; the way it really was, and the emotions were too powerful for him to handle. Here was a veritable time machine, this humble, dog-eared photograph that held the key to his past. It seemed silly, but now he was beginning to realize that this little grainy black and white child *wasn't* someone else; it was *him*. Tears welled in his eyes, as memory after golden memory came flooding back.

219

He opened the car door and took a deep breath. He needed to get a grip.

David stretched his long legs; aching and creaky after the tedious journey, and stood looking at his old school. He hadn't been back to the old place for over twenty years, but surprisingly it still looked exactly the same. He could see the 'David Day Arts and Sciences Block', half obscured by blossom trees, which still made him feel inordinately proud. He felt sure he would be welcome to look around, even if he turned up unannounced, but what he really wanted to do was walk up the high street. He paused at the Zebra crossings and imagined Barbara with her huge arms, beckoning that it was now safe to walk. He crossed over quickly, dodging the horrendously busy traffic that thundered up and down, and wondering what had happened to her. When he was eleven, there were just a handful of cars and buses. Now the air was thick with fumes, but at least the pea-soup fogs had long gone. He walked a few yards up the hill and stood outside what used to be Freddie Fielding's Barbershop. Now it was a dog-grooming parlour. He smiled, as the irony of the situation became apparent, and hoped that the dogs who patronized the place came out looking better than he ever did. The street, bathed in spring sunshine, had looked very different all those years ago, when he left Freddie's shop to walk in the fog. Even the pollution was more picturesque and poetic in those days.

Just up ahead and on the other side of the road was Miss Kettle's shop. His heart pounded as he warily re-crossed the street and made for the front door. The frontage remained the same, but the colouring was much brighter. The shop was now a home furnishings place, with lamps, gilded mirrors, plaster-cast gold cherubs and picture frames, where once were jokes, boiled sweets and toys. David took a deep breath and entered. The doorbell clanged, just as it had done thirty-nine years previously. It was the same old bell. He half expected that no one would answer, but a young lady arrived from the backroom and stood behind the small, grey, lightweight till.

"Can I help you?" she smiled.

"Look," he said, nervously. "Don't think I'm crazy. Do you think I could have a look around the counter, behind the till? It's just for sentimental reasons, you see…"

The lady looked panicky, and said it wasn't allowed. David said that he understood, and walked out, feeling very silly and flustered. He walked on, past where Sammy and Herbert had plotted in the fog, to the lovely old church where his father and mother were married, where he was christened, and where old Miss Kettle was finally laid to rest. For a second, he saw the ghosts of three hundred school children flooding out and heading for home. He could hear the strains of 'All Things Bright and Beautiful' as if it were yesterday.

The shop frontages had all changed now, and a plethora of Balti restaurants had replaced the many butchers' shops. The oak-panelled wool shop and the old-fashioned hardware store, just twenty yards away from each other, were now a tattoo and body-piercing studio and a tattoo removal clinic. The coal yard was gone too, from a town that originally grew around a coal mining quarry. David was approaching the top of the street now, and had lost his bearings. The roads, in his absence, had been completely restructured to cater for the massive amounts of traffic that travelled to the vast Thornwood shopping mall, built to replace the old steel works. For a second, he couldn't remember how to get to his grandparents' old house. He was standing at a road junction with multiple traffic lights and many lanes of screaming cars piloted by youths in baseball caps who didn't look old enough to drive. It was here that he would regularly cross, unaided, at the age of eleven. Now he was fifty, and scared stiff.

Eventually he made it to the other side, and walked a few hundred yards to number fourteen, Thorns Avenue, where Bertha and Reuben had lived. His eyes were once again blurred by unstoppable tears. Both grandparents were long since gone. Reuben gave up smoking too late, and died a horrible death from lung cancer. Ruby had nursed him, promising that he'd soon be back in his beloved garden. Reuben, skeletal and weak, agreed, and smiled at his darling daughter. She was fooling him, as he was fooling her. They both played the game and skirted around the truth, which was far too painful. Bertha died at the age of ninety in a nursing home, so addled by Alzheimer's that she was convinced, near the end, that David was Ruby's husband. She would spend her last days trying to polish the home's many work surfaces, as she had done whilst in service, seventy years before, at the home of the steel works' boss.

David took his little digital camera from his jacket pocket to photograph the old house, but as he was about to do so, a young, heavily-tattooed man emerged and asked what he thought he was doing. David mumbled his apology and walked away quickly. The memories here were just too painful, so he began to walk slowly back down the high street towards his car. He passed the pubs where Bertha, in her heyday, had stood on the tables and sung Ramona, and he passed the old police station, where Sergeant Rhys had ruled with a truncheon of iron.

And what had become of Herbert and Sammy? The intrepid two had teamed up a few years after their earlier failures, and hatched a plan to rob a train in Tipton. There was a shipment of metal on board that fetched a good price at scrap yards and so, in the dead of night, they carted away a ton or so of the stuff from a goods yard in Sammy's van. Deciding that it was best to be patient and let the heat die down, they had hidden their ill-gotten gains in a couple of garden sheds and waited for twenty years - presumably, they got on with something else in the meantime. When they finally thought the time was right, the greying, middle-aged villains reunited and tried to fence the goods, only to be told that the type of metal they had stolen had long since been superseded by a new product, and was, as a result, utterly worthless. The Express and Star newspaper, upon hearing of their exploits, ran a humorous article entitled 'The Not-So-Great Train Robbery.' This must have been especially galling for Herbert and Sammy, as their secret stash of five hundred Beta-max video recorders had also failed to set them up financially. What happened to them after that was anyone's guess. Perhaps they, like Ronald Biggs, fled to Brazil.

Mr Perriman retired not long after the school was saved, and died when David had just turned eighteen. He was asked, along with five other ex-pupils, to carry the coffin at the funeral. Apparently, the head teacher had written it into his will, and even named the ex-pupils he wanted. David was just leaving grammar school, *en-route* to Art College at the time. He was petrified, but knew it had to be done.

Mr Lewis became head teacher and remained so until he retired to Cardiff with his wife, where he eventually died of heart failure. His faithful dog, Lady, died at the age of sixteen, and was buried in their back garden with a headstone, which read:

ALAS, POOR LADY. R.I.P.

May flights of angels sing thee to thy rest.

Mally did not pass his eleven-plus, largely because his letter to the education board, (on cream paper with lapwing illustration) which asked about the possibility of including some questions on taxidermy, had sadly gone unheeded. He saw out his time at the local secondary modern school and became a game warden near Bridgnorth. He and David had drifted apart when they went to separate schools, just as he feared they might. David had often thought about surprising him with a visit when he next visited the area, as he'd heard that Mally had recently suffered a heart attack and needed cheering up. He doubted that he'd even recognize him when he saw him, though of course, he would presumably still have his huge ears.

David's father, Len had died around five years earlier, having lost an awful battle to emphysema. His last year had been spent in a chair, with an oxygen bottle at his side, and suffering dreadful panic attacks. Visits to the local hospital became more and more frequent, and the stays became longer and longer. David and his mother had visited him one Thursday evening, and he had seemed particularly unwell. David had planned to bring along a friend, a professional magician by the name of Chris Priest, to do some tricks for Len in an attempt to raise his spirits. Len loved magic, and often performed simple tricks for his grandchildren, but this little treat had been cancelled at the last minute when the hospital suggested that he didn't seem up to it. At eight o'clock, the sister told Ruby and David that visiting time was over and they reluctantly left him, frightened and alone, to die a few hours later. Len's last words to his son were, "God help me to get through this night." Perhaps that was God's way of answering him. It was David, and not Ruby, who received the call from the hospital at seven the next day, due to an administrative error. His whole world fell apart with that call, and it was left to him to break the dreadful news to Ruby. She wailed her grief back down the phone line, in shock and unable to comprehend life without her man. David, like most men of a certain age, had never told his dad that he loved him, and now he never could. A million memories flooded back, each too painful for him to cope with. He had seen friends who had lost their parents, and they seemed to take it in their stride. Had they not adored their fathers like he had? Were their emotions not as acute? This was the man who had created him, loved him, worried about him when he had a cold, helped with his homework and put him through Art College. He had stood proudly and shed a tear when David had got married, and made his grandchildren wooden toys for their Christmas and birthday presents. He had sacrificed more than David could comprehend to make sure his beloved children and grandchildren were happy, safe and well, and all this was cruelly taken away from him one foul night in a dismal, depressing hospital in Dudley. The man who had loved his family above all else had died frightened and alone at the age of sixty-seven, and David was wracked with mental anguish and guilt.

After a traumatic funeral, Len's ashes were delivered to the house by a kindly man from the funeral directors with a face that looked like it had never been allowed to laugh. He handed over what looked like a plastic sweet jar, just like the ones that Miss Kettle used to have along her top shelf, but in opaque grey. Ruby buried the ashes in her back garden, underneath an ornamental concrete bird bath surrounded by flowers. She had never written anything more than shopping lists in her whole life, but she composed a most eloquent and beautiful letter, sealed it in plastic, and buried it along with his remains. She gave her two sons a copy each, and David, after reading it and weeping bitter tears, filed it away in his studio. Often, whilst searching for something, he would come across the envelope and hastily put it away again unread. He knew that one day he would summon up the courage to open it and read it one more time, when he was feeling strong, or perhaps when its author was reunited with her soul mate in Heaven.

David had been so heartbroken that he became seriously depressed for several years afterwards, wandering around in a daze, unable to concentrate on his work and overwhelmed by a terrible flatness of spirit which took all of his laughter away. He would break down and cry at the most inappropriate times, which must have been a cause of great concern to his family, but these outbursts were necessary and therapeutic to him, if uncomfortable. The tears were his way of releasing some of the pressure that was building inside him, like a valve on a pressure cooker. Without them, the damage would have been even more serious and certainly even longer lasting. After five long years, he could now remember his dad without crying, and even laugh a little at the sillier memories. All he needed was time, but with a father so idolized it took him longer than most.

Ruby was still with him, thank God, and fighting fit, if one excluded the blood pressure, the high cholesterol and the bunions. After the windfall from the British Museum, she had spent a lot of time in Tenbury at the new caravan with her beloved Len, and after he died, she decided to live there, close to her friends from the site, and to David.

And what of the matchbox child?

David was presented with a baby brother, now thirty-nine, and with two children of his own. The pair had been inseparable friends throughout the years, and Paul, for that was his name, (and thankfully not Knighton) had eventually become one of England's most successful playwrights, specializing in both bawdy comedies and poignant dramas, not unlike another local playwright, some four hundred years previously.

Ruby and Len were always curious as to where their sons' talents came from, and often felt like two overworked sparrows trying to satisfy a pair of enormous and demanding cuckoos. Len, in particular, would eye the local milkman with suspicion whenever he saw him off duty, carrying his watercolours and lined notepad.

It was a foregone conclusion that David would go to Art College, and eventually, after many years as a freelance artist, he went on to become a renowned restorer of old paintings and frescos. His work took him to Italy, where he worked on major projects, including Leonardo da Vinci's 'The Last Supper'. If someone had botched a Botticelli, or ripped their Raphael, they called for David. The Italians accepted him and christened him The Day Dreamer - a clever little pun on his surname – because of his occasional habit of staring into space for hours on end when the mood took him.

After a few years of self-employment, when he'd managed to accumulate a few pounds in the bank, David married Suzanne, a Black Country girl whom he had met at college, and after he'd made a name for himself they eventually bought a farmhouse just outside Tenbury Wells. When it came on the market it was very run-down, but he thought that the place might have potential. He and Suzanne were sent the particulars and went to view it, and as soon as they clapped eyes on the property they knew that it was the home they would grow old in. As the estate agent unlocked the front door to show them round, David told Suzanne about the wonderful old farmhouse kitchen that the place had. The agent seemed puzzled, and asked how he could possibly have known about it. David smiled enigmatically and explained that he'd been there before, briefly, in another life.

The majority of the farmland had been sold separately, but the house still had two acres of garden, which was ideal for kids to explore. The couple eventually had two children, Lauren and James, though David had quite fancied naming them Holly and Knighton. Suzanne, however, had quite rightly put her foot down over that one.

The farm had several outbuildings, including an old barn, which David converted to a studio. Another, larger building was duly converted into a home for Ruby, so that she could move out of the caravan, which, like its occupant, was getting a little long in the tooth.

* * *

David, still deep in thought, returned to his car and took one more lingering look at the old school, and then at his precious photograph. He rocked with laughter when he remembered the mad incidents that could only have happened to him - the untold contusions suffered by poor old Miss Kettle before she took over the great toy shop in the sky, the sad demise of his hamsters, Freddie Fielding's Hitler haircuts, the wonderful Shakespeare imbroglio, his plywood flock of sheep, and Charlie the truncheon-happy copper. It all seemed too crazy to have been true, but it

228

certainly was. He reached into the bag of old photos and schoolbooks that his mother had sorted out for him, and found a faded blue exercise book, with 'Geography. David Day. 6L.' written on the front.

He turned it over, and there, joy of joys, was his list. It read:

HAMSTER RESURRECTION

TORNADO

FLOOD

DEATH

EARTHQUAKE

FOG

MURDER

PLAGUE OF LOCUSTS

ANOTHER RESURRECTION

TREASURE

DISASTER

VIRGIN BIRTH

He studied it carefully, and a massive grin appeared across his tear-stained face. Removing his rose-tinted reading glasses and placing them in his jacket pocket, he turned the ignition key, causing the car radio to burst into life. The Beatles were singing 'Help', right on cue. He twisted the key again, started the engine and slowly pulled away from the kerb.

"Nineteen-sixty-five," he said out-loud, to no one in particular. "Now *that* was a good year!"

The End

And a few photographs!

I revisited my old school recently after an absence of some forty-three years, and asked the current head teacher if she'd perchance seen a plywood sheep knocking around. Wishful thinking I know, but worth a try. Imagine my delight when she rang me a week later and told me that she'd spotted the caretaker with a plywood sheep under his arm, heading for the skip. She intercepted him and retrieved it, and now it has been reunited with its tearful, overjoyed owner. You may well laugh, but to me this was better than discovering buried treasure. And you thought my stories were all made up!

Here's the Nativity play, circa 1967. Those lads look awfully young to have that five-o'clock shadow, don't they?

Also, I'm not entirely convinced about the halo above that chap next to Mary. It looks like the kind of thing my dad would have constructed in his shed. Note also that Mary is giving the baby Jesus one of her wary looks, as she doesn't fancy another soaking.

And finally, the school football team of around the time (1963 actually, so a tad earlier). This is included because of the three men at the back. On the left, with the impossibly large hairdo (I'm only jealous, mind) is Ray Weston, the real deputy head of Quarry Bank Junior School when I was there. I changed the name to Brierley Bank to avoid getting myself into trouble, which was rather pointless as I've just confessed all in print! Ray was a wonderful man and still is.

In the middle is the real Mr Lewis, who I adored. Sadly he died aged only 54 of a heart attack. On the right is headmaster, Samuel Perry, another inspirational character. He was a teetotaler and an upstanding Methodist; something I didn't realize when I wrote this story - it was a sheer coincidence! His lovely widow, Gwen, told me when I met her recently. She's ninety-one now and still has a razor-sharp mind, unlike me. I've never had one, mind you!

It was Gwen who lent me these photographs, by the way.

Now, before you go, take a good look at this newspaper cutting – especially the penultimate paragraph. As I said, it was a true story – well, some of it anyway!

Obituary

Death of retired headmaster and church worker

A former headmaster, Mr Samuel Howard Perry, of 42 Timbertree Road, Cradley Heath, died at Hayley Green Hospital on January 17, aged 73.

He leaves a widow Gwen, daughter Lynda and sister Elsie.

During the war he served in North Africa and Italy in the AOP Royal Corps of Signals and in the Army Education Corps.

From 1929 he taught in numerous schools in Rowley Regis, and was headmaster of Quarry Bank Junior School from 1949 to 1973, when he retired.

Mr Perry was a member of Halesowen Probus Club and a lifelong member of Reddal Hill Methodist Church. He served as a Sunday school teacher, superintendent and secretary of the Educational Society.

MANY MOURNERS

The funeral took place at Reddal Hill Methodist Church on January 25. The Rev H. Broadhurst officiated, with readings by Mr R. Raybould.

Organist was Mr E. J. Tromans.

Mourners: widow Gwen, daughter Lynda, sister Elsie, sisters-in-law Dora Perry, Meg Roe, Dorothy Bamford, Christina Goodall, brothers-in-law Ray Bamford and MacDonald Goodall, nieces Christine and Carolyn Perry, nephews Andrew Roe, Nigel Roe, Peter Bayliss (rep brothers John and Paul Bayliss and brother-in-law Clifford Bayliss), Nicholas Youell (rep Alf and Val Youell, brother and sister-in-law), aunts Edith Tromans and Lois Perry, uncle Horace Stevens, cousins Allen and Mary Perry, Dorothy Perry, Ivan Homer, Howard and Mary Perry, Cissy Field, Major and Betty Fellows.

Tom Porter, Rosalind Raybould, Michael Fletcher, Cedric and Christine Randle, Winnie Insall, W. Homer and Ron Clews.

Bearers: Alan Faulkner, Philip Millward, Mervyn Weston, Philip Raybould, Geoffrey Tristram and Ray Weston (ex-pupils of Quarry Bank School).

A full congregation of relatives, friends and representatives attended.

Funeral directors were H. Cope (CH) Limited, Cradley Heath and Dudley Wood.

More books in the David Day Series

MONET TROUBLE

First year art student David Day is persuaded to forge a Monet painting by the mysterious Lord Hickman, but unknown to either of them, several other artists have the same idea.

VINCENT GOUGH'S VAN

An art college murder mystery of Shakespearian proportions, littered with psychic sewing teachers, entrail-painting students and Sapphic assassins.

THE CURSE OF TUTTON COMMON

David sets about trying to improve Britain's worst museum, and ably assisted by a cat named Hitlerina, he discovers an ancient Egyptian tomb in South Staffordshire.

PAINTING BY NUMBERS

Thirty-year-old David is having a mid-life crisis, made worse by the fact that his art studio has exploded, and the ninety-year-old 'paint by numbers' enthusiast he has befriended is not what he seems.

STEALING THE ASHES

Forty–year-old David Day overhears two Australian cricketers plotting to steal the Ashes, and, ably hampered by Laz, he tries his best to thwart their plans.

THE HUNT FOR GRANDDAD'S HEAD

The prequel to Nasty Bump! Daleks have invaded Brierley Bank, but David harnesses their power to see off the neighbourhood bully.

DAVID'S MICHELANGELO

Laz, opens an Italian restaurant with disastrous consequences. Meanwhile, David's dramatic discovery during a trip to Florence promises to rock the art world to its core!

…and two new novels featuring a new hero!

THE CURIOUS TALE OF THE MISSING HOOF

Writer Adam Eve hires a pantomime horse costume, but forfeits his deposit when he loses one of the hooves. His obsessive efforts to locate it create mayhem!

MR. MAORI GOES HOME

Adam Eve's hell-raising uncle has died and left him a substantial amount of money – on condition that he returns a rare Maori carving to New Zealand.

For more information, email gt@geofftristram.co.uk

Those of you who have read a David Day book will know how addictive they can become. At first, you think you can take them or leave them – you are an adult with a modicum of willpower, after all, and no mere book is going to rule your life. Quite soon though, you realize that you've started reading a quick chapter while you're in the bath or the lavatory. From there it is but a short step to the torch under the bed sheets at midnight and the paperback hidden inside your desk at the office. You'll find yourself reading the final chapter extra slowly to make it last longer, savouring every word and even reading good bits twice. Then, when you can stall no further and the book is finished, you will go through an awful mourning process, whereupon an intense craving will kick in. You'll need more and you'll need it NOW. Bad-tempered due to the crippling withdrawal symptoms, you'll probably complain that the author isn't nearly prolific enough for your voracious appetite, and begin to call him rude names. Extreme cases have even been known to try and climb the walls in anguish. Friends will turn against you because you will insist on regurgitating the plots *ad nauseam* while they're trying to watch television. It will get so bad that you might seriously consider a spell in a clinic, or maybe a course of hypnotism.

Well, help is at hand. Why not join the David Day Fan Club? It's a bit like Alcoholics Anonymous. You sit around in a circle and confess, "My name is Deirdre Sponge and I'm a David Day fanatic." (Obviously, you don't say this if your name i*sn't* Deirdre Sponge. That was just an example.) Then the others get up and hug you, with a bit of luck.

If you email me at gt@geofftristram.co.uk I'll keep your name on file and let you know when a new book is due to be released into the wild. Unlike other authors who are now too important – people such as J.K. Rowling and Shakespeare for example, I promise to always be approachable, grateful and humble, and write back. That's with the proviso that you tell me my books are great, of course. I don't want any sour-faced old scrooges writing in to tell me I'm rubbish and that I deserve to be horse-whipped on the steps of my club. Maybe I could cope if you've spotted a glaring error, or a bit you didn't think made perfect sense, but obviously, I'd prefer it if you to told me how a paragraph had made you wet yourself on the train, or prevented you from leaping off a high building to certain death. You can suggest things that David can get up to in future stories, if you wish. I might even write *you* into a book. After all, most of my characters are based on real people, believe it or not!

Anyway, I'll leave it with you. The offer's there. You can lead a horse to water but you can't make it drink, as my Granny Bertha often tried to say. I hope you've enjoyed 'A Nasty Bump on the Head'. It's 'Monet Trouble' next, and if *that* doesn't make you laugh, I'll refund your money.

That was a joke by the way. You have to be so careful in this litigious age. I need the money for a new bathroom - I can't afford to give it back. The bookshops keep forty percent anyway. And another thing. Will you stop lending my books to everyone when you've finished them? Let them buy their own. I'm never going to be another J.K. Rowling at this rate.

Geoff Tristram.